DISTOR FROM THE TRUTH

BY

Richard Henderson

TABLE OF CONTENTS

Table of contents 2

Chapter 1: 5

The Intruder: 5

Chapter 2: 12

The Pursuit 12

Chapter 3: 18

The Descent 18

Chapter 4: 28

Fragments of Reality 28

Chapter 5: 40

Parallel Lives 40

Chapter 6: 52

The Bitter End 52

Chapter 7: 58
Fragile Peace 58

Chapter 8: 61

Three Days Earlier 61

Chapter 9: 65

Two Weeks Ago 65

Chapter 10: 73

The Weight of Confession 73

Chapter 11: 80

The Favor 80

Chapter 12: 87

The World Outside 87

Chapter 13:	90
The Raid	90
Chapter 14:	94
Shadows and Voices	94
Chapter 15:	100
Confrontations	100
Chapter 16:	104
Echoes of the Mind	104
Chapter 17:	106
Morning After	106
Chapter 18:	113
Ghosts from the Past	113
Chapter 19:	120
Point of No Return	120
Chapter 20:	123
The Escape	123
Chapter 21:	129
Transformations	129
Chapter 22:	135
The Escape	135
Chapter 23:	144
The Trout Inn	144
Chapter 24:	152
Blood on the Floor	152
Chapter 25:	158
Exposure	158
Chapter 26:	162

Aftermath 162

Chapter 27: 169

An Unexpected Opportunity 169

Chapter 28: 174

The Ornate Sapphire 174

Chapter 29: 182

The Residents 182

Chapter 30: 193

Fractures 193

Chapter 31: 212

The Unraveling 212

Chapter 32: 222

Into the Abyss 222

Chapter 33: 230

The Final Station 230

Epilogue: 234

Epilogue 2: 236

Acknowledgements: 239

References: 240

Chapter 1:
The Intruder

The London night settled like a shroud over the row of modest flats, bringing with it an eerie silence that seemed to swallow the world whole. Only the distant hum of the city remained, a faint reminder of life continuing elsewhere, terrifyingly far away. Among the identical buildings, one flat stood apart—not in appearance, but in the dim, almost living light that flickered in its upstairs window, pulsing like a heartbeat against the darkness.

Inside that window, Lucy sat perched on the edge of her unmade bed, her frail body hunched forward as if carrying an invisible weight. At twenty-one, she looked both younger and older than her years—her eyes sunken with a fatigue that went beyond physical exhaustion, her skin pale in the opaque glow of her bedside lamp. The room around her existed in a state of controlled chaos: crumpled clothes scattered across the floor like fallen soldiers, half-empty coffee cups balanced precariously atop stacks of open notebooks, pens strewn about as if abandoned mid-thought.

Was this the aftermath of a night spent drowning sorrows, or something deeper, something that had taken root inside her very being? Lucy's gaze fixed on the empty space beside her, where shadows began to shift and coalesce. They gathered mass, taking shape, becoming something—someone—that shouldn't exist. Her heart started accelerating with each passing second. She pressed her palms against her eyes, willing away the apparition forming beside her. Her breath came in shallow bursts, each inhale catching in her throat. 'Why can't I escape?' The thought pounded against her skull.

Her heart hammered against her ribcage, an animal desperate for freedom. Lucy squeezed her eyes shut, every muscle in her body tensing as if preparing for impact. When she opened them again, the world had distorted—colours bleeding into one another, sounds warping. A faint melody played from somewhere she couldn't identify, notes twisting into something sinister as they reached her ears. The figure beside her was no longer merely shadow. It had transformed into something grotesque, its edges blurring and reshaping into a nightmare made flesh. And then it spoke. "It's just us now," it whispered, its voice like fingernails on glass, each syllable scratching against Lucy's sanity. "Please don't..." Lucy's voice emerged as a fragile thread, barely audible even to herself.

Without warning, the figure lunged. A shape of pure darkness swallowed her whole, its weight crushing her against the bed. Lucy felt herself trapped beneath it, her limbs refusing to obey her desperate commands to fight, to flee. Her body trembled uncontrollably, her mind a chorus of denial. 'No, no, no.' The plea repeated in her thoughts, accompanied by hot tears that burned trails down her cheeks.

A flash of crimson caught her attention—the knife that lay on her bedside table, its blade gleaming in the dim light as if offering salvation. With a strength born of pure terror, Lucy stretched her trembling hand toward it, fingers closing around the cool handle. In one fluid motion, born more of instinct than decision, she plunged the knife into the intruder. Again. And again. And again. Each thrust punctuated the silence like a drumbeat, creating a terrible rhythm that echoed against the walls. The figure above her jerked with each impact, its movements growing weaker with each pierce of the blade.

"No!" The word escaped the figure in a gurgle, its voice suddenly, horribly human. And then, stillness. A sudden calm descended upon the room as the figure exhaled its final breath and crumpled beside her. Lucy fell back against the bed, her chest heaving as if she'd run for miles. Her wide eyes fixed on the body now lying motionless on her bedroom floor—no longer a shadowy apparition but a man. Jim. In his thirties, with familiar features now frozen in an expression of shock. A friend. Perhaps something more.

"What have I done?" The words escaped her in a breathless whisper, reality crashing around her like shattered glass. Her hands shook uncontrollably as she stared at them, at the crimson staining her skin. Absolute shock claimed every feature of her face, her mind struggling to process the scene before her—a scene she herself had created. With trembling fingers, she capped the knife and set it aside. Blood dripped slowly from her hands, creating small, perfect circles on the hardwood floor. Her chest rose and fell in an erratic pattern, each breath laced with the metallic taste of fear.

Gradually, her breathing stabilized, but her wide, trembling eyes remained fixed on the sight before her. Jim's body lay twisted at an unnatural angle, the life drained from him by her own hands. As the reality of what she had done began to penetrate the fog of panic, Lucy felt something inside her splinter.

Moving as if in a trance, she grabbed the bedsheet from her unmade bed, her hands shaking so violently she could barely manage the fabric. With frantic, desperate motions, she draped it over Jim's body, her heart pounding a desperate rhythm against her ribs. A chill crept along her spine, a primal instinct urging her to act, to erase the evidence of the horror she had just inflicted. 'I can fix this... I can fix this,' she thought, the words like a prayer in the silent room. Lucy stumbled to the bathroom, her legs nearly giving out beneath her. The person who stared back from the mirror was a stranger—wild-eyed, blood-spattered, fear etched into every line of her face. She splashed cold water against her skin, the shock of it momentarily grounding her in reality. She searched her reflection for answers, for some sign that this was all a terrible dream, but found only naked panic staring back.

With trembling urgency, she scrubbed at her hands under the running water. Blood swirled down the drain in hypnotic patterns, like a lifeline disappearing into an abyss. No matter how hard she scrubbed, no matter how red her skin became from the friction, the stains seemed to linger, marking her, accusing her.

'You... You can't stay here. Just get out. Fuck.'

The thought propelled her back to the bedroom, where her frantic eyes darted around, searching for essentials. She yanked open drawers, sifting through the clutter of her life, pulling on a heavy hoodie and jeans as if new clothes could somehow disguise what she had become.

Her gaze fell on her cell phone, and time seemed to freeze. The screen illuminated with a flurry of texts—misinterpreted dates, Jim's reminders about their planned meeting tonight. Tonight. The night she had ended his life.

With shaking fingers, she grabbed the phone and shoved it into her pocket, the weight of it—of the evidence it contained—nearly choking her.

The hallway felt impossibly narrow as she fled the bedroom, the walls seeming to close in around her with each step. Painted shadows danced at the corners of her vision, taunting her. She glanced back toward the bedroom, where the bedsheet-wrapped figure now seemed more like a macabre illusion than reality.

"You have to leave. Just leave..." she whispered, urging herself forward.

As she approached the front door, her escape route, a sound froze her in place—a loud knock that reverberated through the flat like a gunshot. Her heart raced wildly as another knock followed, the sound of it crawling along her skin.

"Oh God, they heard," she gasped, paralysis claiming her limbs.

Each shadow seemed to lengthen, twisting into grotesque shapes that mirrored the fear gripping her heart. Was that a whisper carried on the wind, or a voice calling her name?. Through the peephole on the front door, she could make out the darkened silhouette of her neighbour, Mrs. Penn—a kind but perpetually curious woman in her sixties. Lucy's breath caught in her throat as Mrs. Penn leaned closer to the door, peering through from the other side with obvious suspicion.

"Lucy? Are you alright, dear?" Mrs. Penn called, her voice muffled but concern evident in every syllable.

Lucy retreated from the door, covering her mouth to stifle her breathing, pretending not to be home. She darted away, rushing back toward the bathroom—the only room without windows facing the street.

The cold tiles pressed against her back as she leaned against the bathroom wall, sliding down until she sat on the floor. The weight of her actions pulled at her like gravity, threatening to crush her completely. In the tense silence, a dripping faucet hissed persistently, the sound of it setting her nerves on edge. Her skin began to crawl as distant, muffled voices reached her ears, blurred and indistinct.

'You killed him. You monster...'

The voice came from nowhere and everywhere, accusatory and harsh.

"Stop! Just stop!" Lucy cried out, pressing her palms against her ears.

'Your neighbour saw you, she saw the blood all over you.' Another voice, different but equally condemning.

Lucy looked down at her hands—still smeared with blood despite her frantic washing. She rushed to the sink, turning the tap to full force and scrubbing at her skin until it burned.

The knocking at the front door continued, more insistent now.

"Lucy? I saw you move in there. Everything okay?" Mrs. Penn's voice carried through the flat, concern now edged with determination.

In a sudden burst of desperation, Lucy darted from the bathroom toward the back door of her flat. She burst into the shared courtyard behind the building, the night air hitting her like a physical blow. Her eyes darted around, searching for any sign that she was being watched, being hunted.

The street beyond the courtyard stretched before her like an uncertain promise. With each step she took, paranoia tightened its grip. Her gaze caught on a man in a hoodie, leaning casually against the corner of a building. His eyes seemed to bore into her, seeing through her disguise to the truth beneath.

'What if he knows?' The thought paralyzed her momentarily. His eyes bored into her, as if he could see the blood staining her hands, the guilt etched on her face. She hunched deeper into her hoodie, wanting to vanish into the shadows.

For a moment, her mind flashed back—not to the horror she had just committed, but to earlier, happier times. Lucy and Jim, laughing together over coffee, the warmth of genuine connection between them. The memory felt so real, so recent.

Had she imagined it all? The attack, the knife, the blood? Had she really killed him?

As the question formed in her mind, the reality of her blood-stained hands answered with brutal clarity.

Chapter 2:
The Pursuit

  A chill swept through Lucy's body, yanking her back to the present moment with ruthless efficiency. Whatever brief respite the memory had provided vanished, replaced by the cold reality of her situation.

  Without further thought, Lucy broke into a sprint, deliberately avoiding the hooded man's penetrating gaze. A primal sense of being watched clawed at her mind, driving her forward with desperate energy. Her feet pounded against the pavement, each footfall echoing with the weight of her actions. The question hammered in her mind with every step: was she running toward something, or away from it?

  The streets blurred around her as she ran blindly, her only goal to put distance between herself and the apartment, between herself and what she had done. The night air stung her lungs, but she welcomed the pain—it was real, tangible, unlike the nightmare that had become her life.

After what felt like miles, a small café shimmered into view, its lights promising a haven she didn't deserve. The bell above the door screamed as she stumbled inside, each chime an accusation. Heads turned, faces morphing into grotesque masks of judgment. The aroma of coffee and cinnamon twisted in her nostrils, becoming the metallic tang of blood.

She squeezed into a booth, the vinyl cold against her sweat-soaked back. Every shadow seemed to lengthen, every whisper a judgment. Her heart hammered a frantic tattoo against her ribs.

'Breathe. Think. They know', a voice hissed in her mind.

Lucy's gaze darted across the room, latching onto faces like a drowning woman grasping for driftwood. The clatter of silverware became a chorus of condemnation. A baby's innocent gurgle morphed into a sinister chuckle. The barista's smile, saccharine sweet, felt like a spotlight illuminating her guilt. Did she see the blood on Lucy's hands, invisible to everyone else?

"Hey there! What can I get you?" the young woman asked, her smile warm and inviting.

Lucy forced her lips into what she hoped resembled a smile, though her face felt stiff and uncooperative.

"Uh... just coffee. Black, please," she managed, her voice sounding distant to her own ears.

As the barista walked away, Lucy's attention was drawn to a man seated at the next table. In his thirties, smartly dressed, he appeared completely engrossed in whatever displayed on his laptop screen. A normal person going about his normal evening, unaware that he shared space with someone who had just committed the unthinkable.

Then, as if sensing her scrutiny, he glanced up, offering a lingering smile that made Lucy's skin crawl. There was something in his eyes—something knowing, predatory. Or was she simply projecting her own fears onto a stranger's innocent gesture?

The barista returned with Lucy's coffee, setting it down carefully on the table. The woman's earlier smile faded as she took in Lucy's pale complexion and trembling hands.

"You okay? You look a little... out of sorts," she asked, genuine concern creasing her brow.

"Y-yeah, um... just a rough night," Lucy replied, willing her voice not to betray her.

The barista nodded, though doubt lingered in her expression. As she walked away, Lucy felt the man's gaze on her again, heavier this time, more deliberate. Her heartbeat accelerated, blood rushing in her ears.

"Don't you think you should tell them?" His voice came as a near whisper, slithering across the space between them.

Lucy stiffened, her pulse racing to a dangerous pace. She looked up sharply, meeting his eyes directly for the first time.

"Are you talking to me?" she demanded, hating the tremor in her voice.

The man didn't answer immediately. He simply held her gaze, his expression unreadable, before finally speaking again.

"Tell them what?..." Lucy pressed, a desperate edge to her question.

"Putting your hands on someone like that... it never ends well."

The words hit her like physical blows. Her stomach dropped, a cold sweat breaking across her skin. She forced herself to look away, pretending she hadn't heard him, pretending her world wasn't collapsing around her.

'Is he... does he know?' The thought ricocheted through her mind, leaving destruction in its wake.

Unable to bear another second under his scrutiny, Lucy bolted from the café, not bothering with her untouched coffee, which spilled across the table and onto her hoodie. She was oblivious to the hot liquid seeping through the fabric as she stumbled onto the dimly lit street, anxiety coursing through her veins like poison.

With no destination in mind, she darted down the nearest alley, putting as much distance as possible between herself and the café, the man, his knowing smile. The darkness enveloped her, but offered no comfort. Instead, the shadows seemed to warp around her, taking on lives of their own. Every sound grew amplified—the scuffle of her own feet against the pavement, a distant shout from the main road, the thunderous sound of her heartbeat echoing in her ears.

Lucy stopped suddenly, bent double as she tried to catch her breath. Her lungs burned, her legs trembled beneath her.

'Just keep moving. No one knows... no one knows...'

The mantra repeated in her mind, a desperate attempt at self-reassurance. But even as she formed the thought, a figure appeared at the alley's entrance—just an unfortunate passerby, likely, but in Lucy's frantic state, a potential threat. She instinctively ducked deeper into the shadows, pressing herself against the cold brick wall, her breath shallow and quick. Lucy overhears a conversation from the other end of the alleyway; "Did you see the state of that woman? Came running out of the café like the devil was after her."

"Yeah, well, they all crack eventually. It's just a matter of time."

"Think she knows?"

"Doesn't matter if she does. They can't prove anything."

The voices were rough, male, and carried a tone that made Lucy's blood run cold. They were close, too close, and she could sense them approaching.

In that pocket of stillness, a fractured memory surfaced—Jim's face hovering above hers, tenderness twisting into something predatory.

'Lucy, you know you'll never forget this, right?' he had purred, his smile a razor's edge.

The image shattered, leaving Lucy gasping in the alley's fetid air. The stench of urine and decay clung to her like a shroud. Her fingers brushed against something slick and cold—a discarded syringe. The brick wall pressed against her back, its surface rough with grime and broken glass. In a shattered mirror, she caught a glimpse of herself—a wild-eyed stranger, smeared with dirt and tears. 'Nowhere to hide.'

Something snapped. A sob tore from her throat, raw and animalistic. She clawed at her face, desperate to peel away the layers of guilt and madness.

Then, footsteps—heavy, deliberate—echoed in the narrow space. Adrenaline surged, twisting her gut.

A figure materialized from the shadows, a man in his forties with a face etched with hard living. His eyes, bloodshot and rheumy, held a flicker of something unsettling—pity? Lust? Amusement? A normal reaction? Lucy was long past normal.

"Hey, hey, are you alright?" he asked, his voice gentle as he took a tentative step forward.

Lucy shook her head violently, panic surging through her veins. "Stay back! Just... just leave me alone!" she shouted, her voice breaking.

The man stepped back, clearly surprised by the vehemence of her response. "I'm just trying to help. You look like you're about to pass out. Do you want me to call someone?"

Lucy scanned her surroundings frantically, looking for an escape route. Her heart pounded so hard she could feel it in her throat, choking her.

His kindness felt like a trap, a way to lure her into a false sense of security before revealing her to the world. She had to get away, before it was too late.

"Just go," Lucy snapped, shrinking back into the shadowed alley.

"Please. I don't want any trouble." The man held up his hands, his voice soft. "Didn't mean to scare you. You look pale, that's all."

She pressed her back into the bricks, eyes darting to the street. "People say that, but it's never just about looking pale, is it?"

"What are you—? I just saw you standing here!" the man protested, clearly bewildered by her reaction.

Hearing the escalating tone of his voice, sensing a threat where perhaps none existed, Lucy bolted past him, her body moving on pure instinct, fuelled by terror and guilt.

Chapter 3:
The Descent

Lucy ran desperately down the street, constantly glancing over her shoulder. The world around her seemed to distort, reality bending at the edges of her vision. Every face she passed felt like an accusation, every pair of eyes a silent judge condemning her for what she had done.

'Can't let anyone in. Can't trust anyone...'

The thought pounded in her mind with each frantic footfall, becoming a mantra, a desperate prayer for survival. Trust had become a luxury she could no longer afford—not when every shadow might hide someone who knew her secret, not when every smile might conceal malicious intent.

Her aimless flight brought her to a bus stop, illuminated by the harsh glow of a streetlamp. For the first time since fleeing her apartment, Lucy paused, a sudden thought cutting through her panic—what if she simply left? Left this place, this city, and these memories behind? Started fresh somewhere no one knew her name, her face, her sins?

With trembling fingers, she pulled out her phone, but hesitated, paralyzed by the fear of making a call. Who would she even contact? Who would help a murderer?

The screen suddenly lit up with a notification, casting an eerie blue light across her face. A text message from Jim. Her breath caught in her throat as she read the words:

'Everything's going according to plan.'

The message sent a jolt of ice through her veins, her mind racing to make sense of it.

'He... he knew. He was coming for me.'

The realization crashed over her like a wave of dread. In her panic, the phone slipped from her grasp, clattering to the pavement where it shattered, the screen splintering into a web of cracks—much like her perception of reality.

Lucy collapsed to her knees, clutching her head in her hands, feeling the last tenuous threads of sanity beginning to unravel. The world tilted and swayed around her, colours bleeding into one another, sounds distorting.

'Shit. I can't stay here, but I can't go back either...'

She raised her eyes to see an oncoming bus, its headlights piercing the darkness like twin knives, illuminating her in their harsh glow. For a brief moment, Lucy considered stepping into their path, ending the nightmare her life had become. Wouldn't that be simpler? A quick end to the guilt, the fear, the uncertainty?

But another thought tugged at her: the thought that she was not in control of her actions. Was she being programmed to end her life? If she stepped in front of the bus, would she be doing it because she wanted to, or because someone else was making her do it? If she died now, she would never know the truth.

But something held her back—not self-preservation, exactly, but a lingering question that refused to be silenced. Had she really killed Jim? The memory felt both vivid and dreamlike, real and unreal simultaneously. If she died now, she would never know the truth.

Instead of boarding the bus, Lucy crossed the street, instinctively seeking the shelter of darkness, blending with the indistinct shadows that haunted the city's edges. She paused, taking one last glance back toward her flat, where a faint light still twinkled from the window. The sight tugged at something within her—a longing for the safety of home, however illusory that safety might be.

'Can I go home...?'

The thought had barely formed when the cacophony of the city was suddenly drowned out by the blaring horn of an oncoming bus—different from the one that had just passed, approaching from the opposite direction. Lucy froze, her feet rooted to the asphalt, her eyes widening with dread as she found herself directly in its path.

Time seemed to slow, stretching like taffy. The bus inched closer, its massive form blocking out everything else, becoming her entire world. The end felt unavoidable, and for a heartbeat, Lucy welcomed it.

Then, without warning, a harsh hand gripped her arm, yanking her out of the vehicle's path with brutal force. She hit the curb hard, scraping her knee and face against the rough asphalt. Pain sparked through her body, raw and immediate, but undeniably real. She was alive.

Lucy scrambled to her feet, breathing heavily, adrenaline coursing through her system. In the cold moonlight, she could finally see her rescuer—a homeless man, perhaps in his fifties, unkempt and wild-eyed, but with a surprising alertness in his gaze.

"Hey, what's wrong with you? You'll get yourself killed," he barked, his voice rough with concern or irritation—Lucy couldn't tell which.

The reality of what had almost happened—what she had almost allowed to happen—hit her like a physical blow. She began to sob into her hands, her body shaking with the force of her grief and guilt.

"Why would you save me? I don't deserve it," she choked out between sobs.

She sank to her knees, her emotions spilling out uncontrollably, raw and unfiltered. In that moment of complete vulnerability, a terrible confession escaped her lips.

"I-I think I killed someone... I can't remember exactly, but I think I did."

The homeless man's expression shifted, a glimmer of something—was it pity?—flashing in his weathered eyes. He hesitated, seeming to waver between empathy and indignation.

"Sometimes the mind plays tricks..." he said finally, his voice softer than before. "Sometimes, it's the drugs talkin'."

He reached into his tattered jacket, producing a chipped crack pipe that caught the moonlight. With a gesture that seemed almost tender, he offered it to her.

"How 'bout you take a hit? It'll help the pain, at least for a moment."

Lucy recoiled instinctively. "No!" she protested, pulling away.

But the homeless man took another step forward, his eyes holding hers. "You're not alone. We all have our demons."

Lucy's breathing quickened as she stared at the pipe, its surface gleaming dully in the dim light. The promise of escape, of numbness, however temporary, beckoned to her with seductive intensity.

"I just want it to stop..." she whispered, her voice barely audible.

The flickering streetlights seemed to dim further, shadows stretching and lengthening around them as the tension thickened. Lucy gazed into the man's bloodshot eyes, her mind spiralling, teetering on the precipice between resistance and surrender.

"Then it'll help, love," he assured her, his voice gentle, understanding.

Lucy stared at the pipe, her resolve crumbling. "Fuck it, I'll do anything to numb this pain."

The homeless man nodded sympathetically. He puffed on the crack pipe first, the ember glowing fiercely in the darkness, before passing it to Lucy. She took it with trembling fingers, raised it to her lips, and inhaled. The smoke scorched her throat, making her cough, but she forced herself to take another drag, desperate for the promised relief.

The effect was almost instantaneous. Vibrant colours exploded around her—a kaleidoscope of swirling hues illuminating the dark void of her surroundings. The cacophony of the city transformed into a euphoric symphony of laughter and warmth that seemed to cradle her in its embrace.

Lucy's eyes widened with wonder, pupils dilating as the drug took hold. "Oh my God, it's beautiful..." she breathed, stretching out her arms as if to embrace the world around her.

.

An ethereal glow surrounded her, and the distant sounds of the city pulsed like a heartbeat, keeping time with her own. She began to twirl, spinning through her vibrant fantasy, the worn asphalt beneath her feet transforming into a lush meadow of wildflowers that caressed her skin as she moved.

"I'm free... I'm finally free!" she cried out, her voice a hymn of liberation.

But the reality was far from the ecstatic vision playing out in Lucy's mind. While she experienced a riot of colours and sensations, anyone watching would have seen only a young woman, dishevelled and distressed, now reduced to dribbling incoherently as she leaned against a homeless man she had just met, her eyes vacant, her movements jerky and uncoordinated.

Even within Lucy's drug-induced euphoria, the illusion proved fragile. The bright colours began to twist grotesquely, warping back into darkness. The joyful laughter that had surrounded her morphed into mocking whispers. Shadows darted at the corners of her vision, creeping toward her with sinister intent.

"What...? No, no... This isn't real!" Lucy cried, confusion and fear replacing the bliss on her face.

The homeless man's features seemed to contort, his expression becoming malevolent. "HA! You thought you could escape?" he jeered, his voice distorted and inhuman.

Lucy stumbled backward, her heart racing. She looked around frantically as the bright colours faded, revealing the grimy reality she had briefly escaped—dirty streets, heaps of trash, and the grizzled faces of other homeless individuals who loitered nearby, watching her with expressions ranging from amusement to predatory interest.

'She thinks she can hide... she thinks she's special!' A voice whispered directly into her mind, followed by cruel laughter.

Lucy clutched her head, desperate to block out the taunts. "Shut up! Just leave me alone!" she shouted, her voice cracking with desperation.

'You can't run from what you've done!' Another voice hissed in her ear, its tone venomous and accusing.

Her fragile grip on reality snapped completely. She turned wildly, searching for the sources of the voices, her eyes darting left and right. In the shadows beyond the pool of streetlight, she caught sight of a figure—ghostly, face obscured, one hand extended toward her in an unmistakable beckoning gesture.

"Get away from me!!" Lucy screamed, lunging forward to strike at the apparition.

Her foot caught on a crack in the pavement. In an instant, she lost her balance, her momentum carrying her forward as everything shifted. Lucy crashed face-first into the unforgiving concrete, the jagged asphalt digging into her cheek with savage intensity.

Pain shot through her body, real and immediate, cutting through the hallucinatory haze. She screamed, the sound tearing from her throat, raw and primal. Struggling upward, she pressed her fingers against her bleeding cheek, catching a glimpse of her reflection in a broken shard of glass nearby.

The bright colours that had filled her vision moments before faded to grey, harsh reality asserting itself once more—her blood mixing with dirt, the remnants of her fevered hallucinations vanishing like morning mist.

"You really gotta get a grip, girl," the homeless man said, now appearing more concerned than menacing, his earlier malevolence revealed as nothing more than a creation of Lucy's drug-addled mind.

From where she sat on the cold pavement, Lucy looked up at him, no longer seeing a villain but a mirror reflecting her own spiral into despair. The voices quieted, leaving only the familiar sounds of the city—blazing horns, an occasional siren wailing in the distance, fragments of laughter drifting on the night air—all starkly real and unyielding.

"Lucy, what have you done..." she whispered, cradling her head in her hands.

Hot, heavy tears cascaded down her dirt-streaked face, mixing with the blood from her scraped cheek. The cold night air stung the wound, grounding her in a reality she could no longer escape.

'You are alone... forever.' The voice was quieter now, but no less devastating in its pronouncement.

Lucy stumbled backward, her legs giving way beneath her as she collapsed onto the cold concrete, feeling it press against her bruised skin.

"Please... someone help me..." she whimpered, her plea lost in the indifferent rumble of the city.

Time blurred. Lucy found herself walking aimlessly through the streets, one hand pressed to her pounding head. The narcotic high had worn off, leaving behind a crushing comedown that slowly transformed into another bout of psychosis.

Jim's voice whispered in her ear, as clear as if he stood beside her: 'You'll rot in prison, murderer.'

"Just stop! Please!" Lucy cried out, unaware that she was speaking aloud, drawing curious and concerned glances from passersby.

'You know the tramp will be easily bribed by a few tinnies and some more crack,' Jim's voice continued, relentless in its accusations.

In Lucy's fractured perception, she was surrounded by bodies—pressing against her, touching her, shouting at her from all sides. In reality, she walked alone, talking to herself in the middle of the road, her distress visible but its cause unknown to those who hurried past, unwilling to get involved.

She passed the homeless man once more—where he leered at her with malicious intent.

"You're a stupid cunt for confessing to a murder," he sneered in her mind's eye. "I'll sell you in for ransom money. I'll be able to find a bed for the next month."

Was this possible? The man was barely conscious, slumped against a wall, too high to communicate, let alone threaten her. But Lucy's paranoia had taken on a life of its own, creating enemies from shadows, threats from silence.

Gripped by a terror that felt as real as the ground beneath her feet, Lucy spotted a loose brick near a construction site. Without conscious thought, her hand closed around it, the rough surface scraping against her palm. She approached the homeless man, her movement's jerky, and mechanical.

The first blow caught him by surprise—a sickening crack as brick met skull. He had no time to defend himself, no chance to escape. The second strike silenced his weak protest. By the third, he was gone, life extinguished like a candle flame in a gale.

But Lucy didn't stop. Couldn't stop. Blow after blow rained down, her arm rising and falling in a terrible rhythm, the brick growing slick with blood. Only when her arm burned with exhaustion did she finally step back, the brick slipping from her numb fingers.

The reality of what she had done hit her with crushing force. Her heart hammered against her ribcage, an animal desperate for freedom. Lucy stared at the man's body—cold, still, drenched in blood and covered with bruises from her unprovoked attack. The man who had saved her life. The man who had, in his own damaged way, tried to help her.

Her breath hitched as the weight of her actions crashed down on her. He was dead because of her. She was a monster.

Lucy's mind spiralled out of control, thoughts fracturing and reforming, lucidity giving way to psychosis and back again. A thousand contradictory ideas about how to cover her tracks, how to escape, how to make this nightmare end, swirled through her consciousness like leaves caught in a violent storm.

Chapter 4:
Fragments of Reality

Lucy began to run toward home, her only thought now to seek refuge in familiar surroundings. She rounded a corner at full speed and collided with someone—the impact nearly sending her sprawling.

"Fucking hell, Lucy, what happened?"

The voice cut through her panic. Maria stood before her, clearly on her way home after a night of clubbing, her makeup slightly smudged, her eyes widening as she took in Lucy's appearance. The alcohol haze that had clung to her friend seemed to evaporate instantly at the sight of Lucy's battered face and wild eyes.

"Oh. Maria? Hi." Lucy's voice came out flat, disconnected from the chaos raging inside her. She attempted to sidestep her friend, desperate to keep moving, to reach the sanctuary of her apartment.

"Hello? Are you just going to walk away from me then? The fuck happened to you?" Maria's tone sharpened with concern and indignation.

Lucy kept walking, forcing Maria to follow. "I fell over on the concrete, no big deal."

"We need to get you to the hospital. Come on, I'll walk you there." Maria reached out to take Lucy's arm, but Lucy jerked away violently, as if her friend's touch might burn her skin.

"I said I'm fine!" Lucy snapped, her voice rising to a shout. "Just fuck off you intrusive cunt, I'll look after myself."

The words hung in the air between them, shocking both women. Maria stood frozen, stunned into silence by the venom in Lucy's voice. Without waiting for a response, Lucy turned and continued her journey home, leaving her friend staring after her with a mixture of hurt and concern etched across her face.

The walk back to her apartment building passed in a haze. Lucy let herself in with her key, her movements' mechanical, divorced from conscious thought. She trudged up the stairs, each step requiring effort, as if gravity had suddenly doubled its pull on her body. At her door, she paused, staring at the familiar wood grain for several long seconds. Taking a deep breath, she exhaled slowly, then slid the key into the lock and pushed the door open.

The apartment that greeted her stole her breath.

There was no sign of a struggle, no overturned furniture, no bloodstains marking the wood floor. And most shocking of all, no body wrapped in her bedsheets. No Jim. No evidence of the violence she was certain she had committed.

Lucy stood in the doorway, her mind struggling to process what she was seeing—or rather, what she wasn't seeing. She moved through the apartment in a daze, checking each room, opening closets, looking under the bed. Nothing. No sign anyone besides her had been here at all.

The realization crashed over her like a wave of ice water: Jim had never been there. There had been no sexual assault, no desperate fight for her life, no knife plunged into flesh. It had all been an intense bout of psychosis—a waking nightmare so vivid she had been unable to distinguish it from reality.

'Yep... that never happened. You fucking crazy psycho.' Jim's voice laughed hysterically in her mind, taunting her with the truth she had been unable to grasp.

A new memory surfaced—what had actually transpired in her bedroom earlier that night. Lucy saw herself lying in bed, eyes wide with terror, stabbing frantically at the air above her while screaming for help. No one had been on top of her. No one had been in the flat at all. Just Lucy, alone with her delusions.

Another flash—the coffee shop she had fled to in panic. She saw herself from an outsider's perspective, sitting alone at a corner table, smiling and giggling at nothing, having an animated conversation with empty air while other patrons watched with worried expressions, exchanging uneasy glances.

'But look in the mirror and in your pocket, sweetheart,' Jim's voice whispered cruelly. 'Some of it was very real.'

Lucy stumbled to the bathroom, dreading what she might find but unable to resist the compulsion to look. The face that stared back at her from the mirror was barely recognizable—battered, bruised, and bloody. Grazes and scratches covered her skin, telling the story of a night spent in violence and fear.

With trembling fingers, she reached into her trouser pocket and pulled out her phone. The display showed the time: 3:07 AM. She quickly navigated to her messages, searching frantically for communications from Jim, but found nothing—no messages, no missed calls, no evidence he had ever contacted her.

As she slid the phone back into her pocket, her fingers brushed against something. She pulled it out and stared in horror at what lay in her palm: part of the homeless man's nose and two teeth, dislodged during her frenzied attack with the brick.

"Jesus!" Lucy clamped her hand over her mouth, bile rising in her throat.

Some parts of the night had been hallucination, but others—the most horrific parts—had been terrifyingly real.

The morning light filtered through closed curtains, casting eerie patterns on the walls of Lucy's bedroom. Tangled in her bedsheets, she stirred and awakened with a sharp gasp, eyes wide with disbelief as memories of the previous night flooded back. Shadows seemed to loom over her, remnants of nightmares flickering at the edges of her consciousness.

Her face—a mask of panic, still smeared with remnants of the night before—was pale and clammy. She clutched the crumpled bedsheets tightly against her chest, drawing her knees up into a fetal position as if trying to shield herself from the world and the truth of what she had done.

'What have I done? What have I done?' The question repeated endlessly in her mind, offering no resolution, only deepening her despair.

With trembling hands, she brushed her hair back from her face, swallowing against the rising tide of nausea. Whispers began to creep into her mind, indistinguishable from her own thoughts at first, then taking on distinct voices.

'We all know what you did, Lucy,' Jim's voice insinuated itself into her consciousness. 'Can you even face yourself?'

'How will you sleep tonight?' another voice added. 'You can't hide from the truth.'

'I'm sure the police have better things to do than investigate a homeless man beaten to death with a brick,' a third voice chimed in, its tone mockingly reassuring. 'Good luck dodging this one.'

Lucy's breathe quickened, and she curled deeper into her makeshift sanctuary, eyes darting around the room as shadows seemed to lengthen and twist into sinister shapes. The walls felt like they were closing in on Lucy.

'You killed me, Lucy,' Jim's voice persisted. 'Do you think you can escape this, monster?'

"Shut up!" Lucy cried out, her voice cracking with desperation. "I didn't—no, I couldn't have!"

She threw the comforter off, scrambling out of bed with hands still shaking uncontrollably. Stumbling toward her bedroom door, she glanced back as if expecting Jim's lifeless body to materialize on her bed.

Lucy rushed into the bathroom, splashing cold water on her face in a futile attempt to wash away the horror of the previous night. The mirror reflected a chaos of dishevelled hair, tear-streaked cheeks, and wide, fearful eyes—a face that felt foreign to her, an unsettling reminder of what she had become.

As she examined her reflection more closely, she noticed bruises forming on her arms. She recoiled at the sight, gasping.

'I'm not a monster. I'm not..'. she thought desperately, trying to convince herself.

'Look at you. Completely unravelling. How cute,' a voice mocked from within her mind.

Lucy locked eyes with her reflection, feeling the edges of her sanity threatening to fray completely.

'What will you do now?' another voice taunted. 'Hide? Live in fear?'

Lucy stumbled back, clutching the edge of the sink for support. Shaking her head vigorously, she attempted to block out the tormenting voices, but they pierced through her defences with terrifying clarity.

"Leave me alone!" she shouted at her reflection, at the voices, at the universe that had conspired to break her.

Suddenly, a loud knock reverberated through the apartment—sharp and unexpected, shattering her already fragile composure. She flinched instinctively, her heart racing as dread wrapped around her like a shroud.

"Lucy? Are you in there? It's Mrs. Penn." The familiar, concerned voice of her neighbour called from the hallway. "I just wanted to check on you, sweetheart."

Lucy froze, feeling trapped. The walls of her small flat seemed to close in around her, the space shrinking with each passing second.

'She knows what you've done,' Jim's voice sneered inside her head.

With shaking hands, Lucy gripped the edge of the counter, battling the war raging within her mind.

She gripped the sink, her knuckles white, fighting the urge to scream. 'They're coming for me. They all know.'

The knocks grew louder, more insistent, pushing her closer to the brink. Lucy's eyes darted around the room, searching for an escape that didn't exist. The usually mundane space of her apartment felt ominous—colours muted, shadows deep and threatening.

In the corner of the room rested a pile of crumpled papers. She caught her breath, heart pounding in her chest as her mind raced with possibilities.

"Shit. I can't let her in," Lucy muttered.

'You're losing it, Lucy,' Jim's voice taunted. 'You're losing your mind.'

Despite her terror, Lucy inched toward the door, trembling fingers poised to unlock it as Mrs. Penn continued her persistent knocking.

"Lucy, sweetheart, please let me in! I'm worried about you!" the older woman called, genuine concern evident in her voice.

A surge of panic ripped through Lucy, her heart racing, battling the urge to respond. Instead, she clenched her jaw, tears spilling down her cheeks as she fought the madness crashing in on her.

"What if I let her in?" Lucy choked on the words. "What if she finds out?"

A thought struck her suddenly—an image of her writing, the scribbled truths that seeped through her manic moments, offering a kind of validation. Could she really face the world with what she had done? Could she confess and find some kind of peace?

'You're already broken,' another voice whispered. 'There's no fixing you now.'

Lucy took a deep breath, steadying herself as much as possible given her state. "No more lies," she murmured, making a decision.

She took a step back, fighting the inner demons gnawing at her sanity, then opened the door just enough to peer through the crack. Warm light from the hallway flooded her vision, stark against the shadows of her mind.

Mrs. Penn stood there, concern palpable in her eyes, holding a plate of cookies—a simple, heartfelt offering of comfort that nearly broke Lucy's fragile composure.

"Lucy? You don't have to do this alone. I'm here for you," Mrs. Penn said softly.

"You shouldn't be here," Lucy replied, her voice barely above a whisper. "I—I hurt someone..."

Mrs. Penn's expression shifted; she leaned closer, perceptive yet cautious, ready to navigate the clearly troubled waters of Lucy's mental state.

"What happened? You can tell me," she encouraged gently.

Lucy felt her walls crumbling, the oppressive grasp of paranoia beginning to loosen, if only slightly. For a moment, she considered unburdening herself, telling this kind woman everything—about the hallucinations, about the homeless man, about the terror that had driven her to violence.

'Maybe... maybe it's time,' she thought.

But at the last second, fear overtook her once more. "Sorry," she said, forcing a weak smile. "I had a lot to drink last night. Talking silly, must still be in my system. I fell over on the way back from town last night, hope I wasn't too noisy and really hope I didn't wake you. Thank you so much for the cookies, apologies again."

Mrs. Penn studied her face for a moment, clearly not entirely convinced by the hastily constructed explanation. "Okay, dearie, no need to apologize. I'm here when you are ready to talk."

With that, the older woman turned and walked back to her own apartment. Lucy shut her door quickly, turning the lock with shaking fingers.

As soon as Mrs. Penn was gone, paranoia gripped Lucy again. The voices in her head swelled in volume, mocking her attempted deception, their taunts feeding the psychosis taking hold once more.

The silence was worse than the knocking. She was alone with her thoughts, and they were turning on her. 'She knows, she's calling the police right now.'

Lucy began pacing around her flat, her breath quickening, frantically talking back to the voices that tormented her.

"You're wrong! You're wrong! I know you're not real!" she pleaded, clasping her hands over her ears as if that could somehow silence the voices inside her head.

The air around her seemed to thicken with tension; the room began to warp and shift as Lucy's grip on reality faltered once more. She suddenly saw figures inside her flat—blurred, indistinct shapes hovering at the edges of her vision. Though some part of her remained aware they weren't real, their presence intensified her fear. She broke down, crying uncontrollably, sinking to her knees on the floor.

'Poor old lady,' a voice mocked. 'I think she knows how disgusting you really are.'

The multiple voices began talking over each other in unrecognizable dialects, creating a cacophony in Lucy's mind. Then, in the midst of this chaos, Jim reappeared. He stood before her, mocking her with a twisted grin, his presence more menacing than ever.

'Can you feel it building, Lucy?' he taunted, his voice rising and falling in an eerie rhythm. 'The pressure, the fear, the inevitable break? They're all waiting for the show to begin!'

Lucy's perception exploded into a kaleidoscope of colours—pinks, purples, yellows—each hue vibrant yet disorienting. Although the colours were bright, almost beautiful in their intensity, Lucy's fear remained palpable as she struggled to navigate this hallucinatory landscape.

His laughter echoed through her mind, distorting into something inhuman, something that spoke to her deepest fears. 'You can't hide from what you are,' he sang, his voice taking on an almost melodic quality that made his words even more terrifying. 'You can't escape what's coming!'

She stumbled forward, colliding with a wall, the impact briefly shifting her perception from hallucination back to harsh reality. It happened again as she staggered in another direction, crashing into the wall once more, the bright colours flaring back to life around her after each momentary return to clarity.

Finally, as the psychotic episode began to wane, Lucy crumpled onto the floor, curling herself into a fetal position. In the heavy silence that followed, a notification sound from her phone cut through the quiet like a knife.

The screen lit up, revealing a text message from Maria: "We need to talk! Can I come over?"

Fresh panic sharpened Lucy's features as she dropped the phone. She sank down to the floor, hugging her knees tightly, rocking back and forth in a futile attempt to self-soothe.

"Does she know?" Lucy gasped, breathing heavily. "This isn't real, this isn't real..."

The voices in her head amplified once more, flooding her mind like a cacophony that drowned out all reason.

'They're going to get you!' they chanted in unison.

'Yeah, she wants to come round for a brew and a catch up,' a female voice added sarcastically. 'Nothing to do with being smothered in blood and bruises, 100 yards from a man with half his face missing!'

'How long do you think you get for unprovoked murder in the street?' a male voice questioned coldly.

Lucy stared blankly at the text on her phone, her panic rising as Maria sent a follow-up question mark after her message remained unanswered. Her heart pounded against her ribs as she forced herself to type a response.

"Now isn't a good time."

Maria replied almost immediately, the speed of her response adding to Lucy's mounting anxiety.

"I don't know what's going on with you, but we need to talk about last night. Are you at home?"

Lucy looked gripped with fear, her thoughts spiralling in ever-tightening circles. She debated whether to respond at all, her fingers hovering over the screen indecisively. After a moment of hesitation, she typed a single word:

"No."

Maria read the message but didn't respond. Lucy watched the screen, feeling suffocated by the silence that followed. Panic surged through her veins once more, propelling her to her feet. She began pacing frantically around her flat, unable to stay still as the voices in her head rose in unison, mocking her feeble attempts at control.

'Do you think she's stupid? This isn't over, hahahaha!' they taunted mercilessly. 'Maybe she just wants to give you a kiss and a cuddle. You looked in distress! She knows where you live. She's round the corner. You know she'll come anyway, hahaha!'

As her anxiety mounted, Lucy's surroundings began to twist under the weight of her psychosis. The walls of her flat seemed to melt and reform, transforming her once-safe haven into the grimy alleyway where she had committed the unthinkable act just hours before.

CHAPTER 5:
PARALLEL LIVES

In another part of London, as Lucy's world disintegrated into chaos, a man named Peter was just beginning his day. The morning light filtered through half-drawn blinds, illuminating a dishevelled bedroom as the camera slowly panned across the cluttered space before settling on a man in his late twenties.

Peter woke with a grunt, disorientation evident as he stretched and swung his legs over the side of the bed. Standing, he approached the mirror on the wall, his gaze critical as he examined his reflection. A flash of arrogance crossed his features as he noted a hint of definition in his chest and torso—the remnants of a once-athletic build. The fleeting smirk was short-lived, however, replaced by a grimace as he turned to the side, and confronted by the prominent beer gut that hung over the waistband of his boxers.

With a sigh of resignation, Peter shuffled into the kitchen, his movements sluggish from sleep and the lingering effects of the previous night's excesses. He reached into the refrigerator and grabbed a can of beer, cracking it open with a dull sound that echoed in the quiet apartment. He took a long swig as he wandered into the living room.

There, he sat heavily at the coffee table where four neatly lined rows of cocaine awaited him. The weight of his choices pressed down on him, visible in the slump of his shoulders, yet he reached for the first line without hesitation. He snorted it with a quick inhale, following it immediately with another deep gulp from his beer can.

As he leaned back against the couch, his phone buzzed with notifications. The screen revealed a dating app filled with a list of messages he had sent—all without reply—to various women. Undeterred by the previous rejections, he began typing the same generic opener to multiple new matches: "Hi how are you x". He swiped through a few more profiles, a familiar emptiness settling in. 'Another face, another potential disappointment. What's the point?' He almost deleted the app entirely, a fleeting thought of embracing the void

But before he could send more than a few, a pop-up interrupted his routine: "MAXIMUM DAILY CONVERSATIONS REACHED. CAN ONLY CONTACT 55 WOMEN EVERY 24 HOURS."

Frustration clouded his features as he exhaled heavily, the sound filled with disillusionment and resignation. The phone screen displayed the time and date: 10:30 AM TUE.

Peter rose from the couch and approached the window, peering out at the world beyond the confines of his apartment. His expression darkened as he surveyed the grim block of flats below, walls smattered with graffiti and windows adorned with England flags. As he watched, a Pakistani boy crossing the concrete courtyard was suddenly accosted by a group of older teens, their racial slurs audible even from Peter's vantage point.

'The moronic gestures of the many outweigh the views of the few, he thought bitterly. Well, it's like that round here anyhow. Poor cunts don't deserve that, but why should I care? I've got my own shit existence to figure out, oh the fucking joys.'

He abruptly drew the curtain closed, blocking the scene from view but not from mind. 'Hope is a powerful thing; too much can kill you and break your heart. But when your life seems devoid of delusion, what then? A feeling beyond the futility of pure nothingness.' The thought lingered as he turned back to face his empty apartment, the silence broken only by the distant sounds of the estate and the persistent buzz of his phone, still offering the hollow promise of connection.

He turned back to face his empty apartment, the silence broken only by the distant sounds of the estate and the persistent buzz of his phone, still offering the hollow promise of connection. He knew he should get ready for work, but the thought of facing another day of meaningless tasks felt overwhelming. 'What's the point?' he thought bitterly. 'Just another day of pushing papers and pretending to care about things that don't matter.'

Meanwhile, in her flat across the city, Lucy remained trapped in her own mind, her reality fracturing further with each passing minute. The stark contrast between her descent into madness and Peter's numb existence formed a strange parallel—two lives spiralling in different ways, yet connected by the thread of isolation that ran through both their stories.

As Lucy cowered on her floor, the voices in her head growing louder, and Peter stared blankly at his reflection, contemplating another line of cocaine, neither could know how their paths would eventually intersect, changing both their lives forever.

In Lucy's fractured reality, the walls of her flat had completely disappeared, replaced by the grimy alleyway she encountered earlier. She sat back down on what she perceived as cold, wet concrete, clutching her knees to her chest once more, trying to make herself as small as possible.

Suddenly, a prison warden materialized before her, his uniform crisp despite the squalid surroundings. He banged a truncheon against a metal bin, the scent of disinfectant and stale sweat rising from the damp concrete floor. The sound echoed through her mind with a harsh, reverberating BANG that made her flinch.

As she cowered from the imaginary guard, Lucy's gaze drifted to a dark corner of the alleyway, where a dirty, diseased rat scurried along the wall. Rather than feeling revulsion or fear, she experienced an odd sense of comfort at the sight of the creature. In her warped perception, the rat represented innocence—a being that simply existed, neither judging nor condemning her actions.

Lucy reached out with trembling fingers, then the rat approached, allowing her to stroke its matted fur. The small creature nibbled at her face in what she interpreted as a bizarre semblance of affection. Lucy found herself seeking solace in this moment of connection, despite the chaos raging around and within her.

With a violent jerk, the scene shifted back to reality. Lucy found herself sprawled on the floor of her living room, hugging a dirty towel to her chest. The rat, the alleyway, the prison warden—all figments of her fractured mind.

As the psychotic episode eased momentarily, Lucy struggled to her feet, her legs weak and unsteady beneath her. She shuffled into the kitchen, visibly shaking from exhaustion and the lingering effects of the crack cocaine.

She reached for a glass and filled it with water from the tap, her hand trembling so violently that the water splashed over the sides. As she lifted the glass to her parched lips, it slipped from her grasp and shattered across the floor, sending glass shards and water in all directions.

Lucy gasped, her heart racing again at the sudden noise. With mechanical movements, she grabbed a dustpan and brush from under the sink and began cleaning up the broken glass, methodically sweeping each shard into the pan before discarding it in the bin. She mopped up the spilled water with kitchen roll, her movements slow but deliberate.

Determined not to be defeated by something as simple as getting a drink, she filled another pint glass, still trembling. This time, she steadied herself with both hands, bringing the glass carefully to her lips. The cool water soothed her raw throat, a small mercy in the hellscape her life had become.

Time passed indeterminately in the flat. Lucy had drawn the curtains, plunging the space into a twilight gloom that matched her mental state. The silence that had settled was suddenly shattered by a sharp knock at the door.

Panic washed over Lucy's face as she froze, hoping that if she remained perfectly still, whoever was outside would assume the flat was empty and leave. But another knock followed, this one more insistent, accompanied by a familiar voice.

"I know you're in there; we need to talk!" Maria called through the door, her tone leaving no room for evasion.

Lucy hesitated, then crept toward the door on unsteady legs. After a moment's internal debate, she pulled it open and yanked Maria inside quickly, her eyes darting up and down the hallway for potential observers before shutting and locking the door behind them.

"Give me a minute," Lucy said, her voice hoarse. "Just... sit down for a sec. Okay?"

Without waiting for a response, she rushed to the kitchen, her whole arm shaking as she filled the electric kettle. With trembling hands, she closed the lid and switched it on, the familiar routine of making tea providing a momentary anchor to normality.

When Lucy returned to the living room moments later, Maria was perched on the edge of the sofa, her posture tense, and eyes watchful. Lucy placed two mugs on the coffee table before sitting beside her, careful to maintain some distance. The atmosphere was heavy with unspoken tension, questions hanging in the air between them.

Lucy's body continued to tremble, the cuts and bruises from the previous night still painfully visible. Maria placed a hand gently on Lucy's leg, an attempt to offer comfort that made Lucy flinch slightly at the contact.

"What's going on with you?" Maria asked, her voice softer than it had been at the door, but still direct.

"What do you mean? Going on with me?" Lucy fidgeted with the sleeve of her sweater, avoiding Maria's gaze.

"Well, there's a lot to unpack," Maria said steadfastly. "For now, I'll ignore how you talked to me last night. But just in general, you haven't reached out in forever?"

"I'm really sorry about that," Lucy replied, her voice small and contrite. "I'm just not myself at the moment."

"No shit..." Maria muttered, eyeing the bruises on Lucy's face with concern.

"I think I got a concussion from falling over," Lucy offered weakly, attempting to deflect.

Maria's expression hardened slightly. "Oh really? And it's a coincidence that you're battered and bruised, and 100 yards down the road from you was a tramp who looks like he had half his face missing?"

Lucy stared blankly at her friend, the words hitting her like physical blows. Had Maria somehow seen what she'd done? Did she know? The thought sent a fresh wave of panic through her system.

'It often helps to imagine people naked to have something else to focus on,' Jim's voice suggested in her mind, inappropriate as ever.

Lucy blinked, and when she opened her eyes, her perception had shifted once more. Maria was sitting before her, now topless and in her underwear, though in reality her friend remained fully clothed. Lucy's paranoia momentarily faded as her attention drifted to this hallucinatory version of Maria's body.

As the real Maria continued speaking, her tone shifted from calm to frustrated, clearly upset that Lucy was zoning out instead of paying attention. However, to Lucy, all of Maria's words became inaudible, drowned out by the rushing of blood in her ears and her own internal thoughts.

Lucy's gaze lingered on the hallucinated version of her friend, her heart racing as she contemplated feelings she had never acknowledged before. Suddenly, she felt a rush of attraction to Maria, the intensity of her anger becoming oddly alluring in Lucy's distorted perception.

In her mind, Lucy's imagination spiralled as she envisioned Maria yelling and then playfully pulling her close, gripping her tightly. The fantasy shifted to an intense scene where Maria was both angry and affectionate, overwhelming Lucy's senses with conflicting emotions.

Caught in this daydream, untethered from reality, Lucy leaned forward impulsively, taking a chance. She pressed her lips against Maria's in a kiss that existed only half in reality—a genuine physical action motivated by a completely hallucinatory context.

Reality crashed back in like a tidal wave. Maria was fully clothed and fuelled with fury at the unexpected advance. She reacted instinctively and with surprising force.

In a swift motion, Maria's fist connected with Lucy's face, punching her square in the nose. Blood spurted instantly, the bright crimson a stark contrast against Lucy's pale skin.

"What the fuck is wrong with you?!" Maria shouted, already on her feet and backing toward the door.

Lucy clutched her nose, wincing in pain as Maria stormed out of the flat, the door slamming behind her with a finality that echoed through the empty rooms.

Left alone once more, Lucy remained kneeling on the floor, one hand pressed against her bleeding nose, blood trickling down her wrist and staining her sleeve. The pain was sharp but oddly grounding; it pulled her momentarily away from the chaotic thoughts that had been swirling in her mind.

Her eyes darted around the room, scanning the walls adorned with photographs from better times—images of laughter and friendship that now seemed to belong to another person's life entirely. She rose slowly to her feet, still trembling from the encounter and its violent conclusion.

The voices returned almost immediately, whispering and hissing, swirling through her mind like smoke from a fire that refused to die.

'You ruined that like you ruin everything! She'll never come back! You're alone, forever!' they taunted in unison.

Lucy gripped her hair tightly in frustration, squeezing her eyes shut as if trying to physically block out the tormenting voices. She sank onto the couch, her body slack with defeat.

The blood from her nose continued to trickle, dribbling onto the fabric of the sofa. But rather than panic at the stain, she found a twisted comfort in the pain—it was real, tangible, unlike the shadows and whispers that haunted her.

She noticed a small mirror on the coffee table and picked it up, staring into her reflection. Her face was smeared with blood, eyes wide and hollow, ringed with dark circles that spoke of sleepless nights and days filled with dread.

Lucy shifted her gaze away from the mirror and instead focused on her hands, which continued to tremble uncontrollably. She swallowed hard, fighting back a wave of emotion threatening to overwhelm her.

'What's the point?' She thought, a profound weariness settling over her.

She reached behind her to retrieve her phone from where it had fallen on the couch, its screen reflecting her dishevelled state when it lit up. She unlocked it, trying to compose a message to Maria, but found herself paralyzed by the torrent of thoughts racing through her mind.

Her heart beat faster as she scrolled through her contacts; each name felt like a reminder of her isolation, of friendships neglected or destroyed. She stopped at Maria's name and hesitated, thumb hovering over the screen.

"I'm sorry..." she whispered to the empty room.

She began typing slowly, pausing between each word, and her heart pounding louder with each stroke of her thumb against the glass screen.

"I don't know what's wrong with me. I'm sorry for earlier. I need help."

Lucy's finger hovered over the send button, uncertainty weighing heavily in her chest. Just before she could press it, the voices rose in an angry crescendo, drowning out her own thoughts.

'Help? You think anyone can help?' they mocked cruelly. 'You don't deserve it! Just cut it out. It's easier that way!'

Lucy's breath quickened, her chest tightening as she dropped the phone onto the couch cushion beside her. She scooted back until her spine pressed against the wall, feeling its solid support anchoring her to reality.

"I'm not listening to you," she muttered defiantly, though her voice lacked conviction.

The shadows in the room seemed to twist and morph into grotesque forms before her eyes, towering over her, taunting grins stretching across their formless faces. As panic consumed her, she felt an overwhelming numbness settling in, slowly wrapping around her heart like cold chains—disabling her from feeling even the simplest ache of despair.

'Maybe its better this way,' she thought. 'Maybe it is just... easier.'

She closed her eyes tightly, her breathing shallow and rapid. Moments stretched eternally as she sat in the cocoon of silence, teetering on the edge of isolation and despair, drowning in the dark currents of her own thoughts.

The sudden whistle of the kettle from the kitchen sliced through the tense atmosphere, startling her. The sound seemed oddly distant, as if coming from another world entirely. Slowly, Lucy uncurled herself from the wall, moving like a marionette pulled to life by unseen strings.

She dragged herself to the kitchen, hands still shaking from the aftermath of the confrontation. She poured hot water into a mug, staring blankly as steam spiralled into the air, dissipating against the ceiling.

As she stood there, Maria's furious words replayed in her head, each sentence twisting like a knife in her gut: 'What the fuck is wrong with you?!'

Something shifted within her; a small voice of vulnerability seeped through the numbness that had enveloped her. With an unsteady hand, she picked up her phone again from where she had left it on the couch.

This time, she scrolled through her contacts not with fear, but with desperation. Her resolve faltered momentarily, but Lucy took a shaky breath, and for the first time in what felt like an eternity, she began to feel the tiniest glimmer of hope, intertwined with the agony of recognizing how far she had fallen.

She pressed send on the message she had composed earlier, then added another:

"Please come back. I need you."

Lucy stood at the counter, her heart pounding in her chest, anxiety gripping her as she watched her phone with bated breath. The screen showed Maria was typing, the three dots pulsing hypnotically.

Finally, the reply appeared:

"I don't know what is going on with you but I need time. Please don't message me until I'm ready. We'll talk about everything when I'm ready. I'm sorry for how I handled that and hope your nose isn't broken."

Lucy read the message, dread pooling in her stomach. She stared at the phone, frozen with shame and regret, the finality of Maria's words settling over her like a shroud.

After a long moment, she opened a kitchen drawer and placed her phone inside, shutting it away from her sight. Out of sight, but not out of mind just like the consequences of her actions that continued to haunt her, whether she could see them or not.

Chapter 6:
The Bitter End

Lucy walked back into the living room and crashed onto the sofa, all energy drained from her body. A suffocating numbness enveloped her, different from the chaotic terror of her hallucinations—this was emptiness, a void where emotion should be. The room was eerily quiet, almost serene in its stillness.

Suddenly, the rat reappeared next to her—an echo of the bizarre comfort she had found in its presence. She clutched at the rat, holding it to her chest as tears began to flow unbidden down her cheeks.

She started to cry, her sobs quiet but wracking her entire frame. There were no mocking voices to torment her now; just an overwhelming silence that gave space to the emptiness inside her, making it feel vast and insurmountable.

As Lucy's sobs gradually subsided, a wave of humiliation washed over her—she felt exposed and fragile, stripped of all defences. The memory of how she had assaulted Maria, misreading the situation so completely, made her cringe with shame.

'What have I done...?' The thought echoed in the hollow chambers of her mind.

Without warning, the ambient silence shattered, replaced by a cacophony of laughter. The room around her morphed into a circus atmosphere, grotesque in its whimsy. Colourful lights spun wildly across the walls, shadows dancing and mocking her vulnerability.

'That went well!' the voices jeered in unison. 'So desperate to feel wanted, it's fucking pathetic!'

The laughter grew louder as Jim materialized before her, dressed in a comical outfit—a clown with exaggerated features, his face painted with a leering smile. He smirked, shaking his head in theatrical disbelief.

'Look at you, Lucy!' he exclaimed, his tone cheerful but laced with cruelty. 'You wanted to be the hero, but you've become the joke! It's funny, really. It all started when you thought I'd assaulted you... and now, well...'

The laughter intensified, echoing painfully in her mind as Jim gestured around the room with exaggerated movements.

'Now you've forced yourself on someone else, and how'd that work out for you? Punched in the face! Classic!' he cackled, slapping his knee in mock hilarity.

Lucy's expression hardened, humiliation transforming into paranoia. The vibrant colours in her vision began to drain away, the whimsical circus scene fading into shades of black and grey that resembled the grimy alleyway she encountered earlier.

Another figure emerged from the shadows: the prison warden from her earlier visions, his uniform now unmistakable. He banged his truncheon against a metal bin, the sound discordant and unrelenting, and each strike sending a jolt through Lucy's overwrought nervous system.

'You're going to prison!' the voices warned. 'What if Maria tells the police? What if she reports you for touching her?'

Lucy's breath quickened as paranoia gripped her tightly. She backed away from the imaginary figures, trying desperately to escape the thoughts that clawed at what remained of her sanity.

She stumbled blindly toward the kitchen, disoriented and losing track of her surroundings. In her panic, she crashed into the wall, the impact causing her nose—already tender from Maria's punch—to begin bleeding again.

Lucy glanced down, seeing blood pooling around her face, but she couldn't focus on the physical pain. Instead, she felt the constricting grasp of fear tightening around her throat, choking off rational thought.

Slowly, cautiously, she felt her way along the wall until she reached the cupboard where she had hidden her phone. With trembling hands, she retrieved it and turned it back on, the screen illuminating her blood-streaked face in the dim light.

She scrolled to Maria's contact, only to discover she had been blocked. The final lifeline she had desperately reached for had been severed.

Her world collapsed further, whatever fragile hope she had maintained disintegrating entirely.

"No... No, no, no..." she whispered, her voice barely audible.

Lucy slid down the wall, her body curling into a fetal position on the kitchen floor. The vibrant colours that had briefly returned to her world faded once more into dullness, her spirit sinking deeper into the abyss of despair.

Later—Lucy had no idea how much time had passed—she found herself still curled on the floor, her body language screaming defeat to an empty room.

"I can't do this anymore..." she whispered, her voice hollow and defeated.

She closed her eyes tightly, exhaustion weighing down her body like a physical burden. Desperation seeped into her voice as she called out to the one constant presence in her fractured reality.

"Jim, just... just kill me. Please..." she sobbed, no longer caring how pathetic she sounded.

The shadows shifted, and Jim reappeared, though his form seemed less menacing than before. He looked at Lucy with an expression that appeared almost sympathetic, his tone softer, almost comforting.

'Not today, Lucy,' he said gently. 'You aren't alone in this.'

He moved closer, crouching beside her on the floor. He reached out, his imaginary hand hovering near her face as if attempting to calm her frantic breaths.

'I can't say it'll be okay...' he continued, his voice sincere. 'But you aren't alone. I'm here to the bitter end.'

Jim snuggled against her, pulling her into an embrace. Lucy's body trembled as she let the floodgates open fully, weeping in the arms of a phantom, seeking solace from a figment of her own fractured mind.

"I just want it all to end..." she whispered between sobs.

In the background, she heard a haunting melody about eternal rest which begin to play—whether from her stereo or her imagination, she couldn't tell. The melancholy tune wrapped around her like a shroud, its lyrics about escaping into peaceful sleep resonating with her desperate state.

As the music swelled around her, Lucy reached once more for her phone, desperation coursing through her veins. She hesitated briefly before signing onto an old dating app she hadn't used in ages, seeking any form of human connection that might pull her back from the brink.

Her eyes widened as she saw the hundreds of unread messages that had accumulated during her absence from the platform. With a trembling finger, she clicked on the topmost notification, from someone named PETE011.

"Hi, how are you? x"

The message was simple, generic even—the kind of opening line sent to dozens of women by men casting wide nets in the digital dating pool. But to Lucy, in that moment, it represented something else: a potential lifeline, a connection to the world outside her disintegrating mind.

Across London, in his dimly lit flat, Peter lay alone in bed, his expression a mixture of self-loathing and despair. The cocaine high had worn off hours ago, leaving him in the familiar trough of his daily cycle—artificial euphoria followed by crushing emptiness.

'What the fuck is wrong with me?' He thought bitterly. 'Why do I continue this pitiful existence? Hope was extinguished a long time ago...'

He turned onto his side, heart heavy with self-disgust, eyes fixed on the peeling wallpaper across from his bed.

'I'm such a coward,' the thought continued, merciless in its assessment. 'Every day I don't drive my car into a wall is further proof of my weakness of character. One day it'll all be over, and it'll be like I never existed.'

A notification sound broke the silence, cutting through the darkness lingering in his mind. Peter glanced at his phone, expecting nothing of consequence—perhaps another app notification designed to lure him back to mindless scrolling.

Instead, his heart quickened as he saw a reply notification from one of the countless women he had messaged on the dating app. someone named Lucy had actually responded.

"Hi... Are you there?"

In the emptiness of his flat, Peter stared at the message, his finger hovering over the screen. Two lost souls, each at the end of their rope, reaching blindly into the digital void—unaware that their connection might become either salvation or the final push into the abyss.

CHAPTER 7:
FRAGILE PEACE

Morning sunlight filtered through the thin curtains of Lucy's bedroom, casting a warm glow across the tangled sheets where she and Peter lay nestled together. The soft notes of a melancholy song drifted from Lucy's small speaker, creating a cocoon of intimacy around them. In this moment, the demons that had haunted Lucy seemed mercifully distant, held at bay by Peter's presence.

They shared a playful glance before Lucy leaned in, pressing her lips against his in a tender kiss that quickly deepened, leading to an intimate connection that temporarily erased the chaos of the previous weeks. Afterward, they lay close together, limbs intertwined, lost in their own world of newfound comfort.

"I could stay like this forever," Lucy murmured, a genuine smile softening her features for what felt like the first time in ages.

The sudden knock at the door shattered their peaceful bubble. They exchanged glances, their smiles lingering despite the interruption.

"Could you get that for me?" Lucy asked playfully, pulling the sheet up to cover herself.

Peter nodded, quickly throwing on a T-shirt and boxer shorts before ambling to the front door. His footsteps padded across the hardwood floor, each step taking him farther from their sanctuary.

When Peter opened the door, he found himself face-to-face with a police officer—a man in his forties with a stern but calm demeanour that immediately set Peter on edge.

"Can I help you, officer?" Peter asked, confusion evident in his voice.

The policeman's gaze was steady, professional. "Is Lucy in?"

"Uh, she's out right now," Peter lied instinctively, sensing danger. "I'm house sitting."

The officer studied him closely for a moment, clearly weighing the truth of his statement. "I can't discuss details of an ongoing investigation, but Lucy may be a potential suspect. We'd like to have a chat down at the station to clarify her involvement."

A cold knot of anxiety formed in Peter's stomach. "Sure, I'll pass on the message," he managed to say, keeping his expression neutral.

He closed the door and stood there for a moment, processing what had just happened before walking back to the bedroom, his mind racing with questions. As Peter walked back to the bedroom, his mind was a whirlwind of conflicting thoughts. "What have I gotten myself into?" he wondered. "This girl is trouble. Serious trouble. I should just walk away, cut my losses, and forget I ever met her."

But then he thought of Lucy's face—her vulnerability, her fear, her desperate need for help. "No," he said aloud, "I can't do that. And besides... what else do I have to lose?" A dark smile crossed his lips. "Maybe this is exactly what I need. A chance to burn it all down and start over. Or maybe just burn it all down."

Lucy was still in bed when he returned, smiling at him expectantly. The expression froze on her face when she saw the concern etched across his features.

"What was that about?" Peter asked, his voice quiet but tense. "Why was there a policeman looking for you?"

Lucy's face drained of colour, anxiety washing over her features like a tide. She opened her mouth to speak, but no words came out.

Chapter 8:
Three Days Earlier

Three days before the police officer's visit, Lucy and Peter lay in the same bed, bodies close, both looking remarkably relaxed given the tumultuous circumstances that had brought them together. The atmosphere between them was intimate, a fragile connection forming in the aftermath of their individual struggles.

"I feel so safe with you, Peter," Lucy confessed softly, surprising herself with the admission. "You're just what I needed right now."

Peter gave her a reassuring smile, listening intently without interrupting. Something about his quiet presence invited confidence, allowing her to lower her guard in a way she hadn't with anyone in a long time.

Lucy's expression grew more serious as she continued. "Things have been horrific lately..."

Peter nodded, clearly unsure how to respond but willing to hear whatever she needed to share. Lucy took a deep breath, feeling the mood shift as memories surfaced that she had spent years trying to suppress.

"I never expected that day to change my life forever," she began, her voice trembling slightly.

Peter listened intently; his expression carefully neutral. He'd heard stories like this before—trauma, loss, mental illness. Everyone had their baggage. But something about Lucy's voice, the tremor in her hands, suggested this was different. 'She's really broken.' A disturbing thought occurred to him. 'Does that make me a bad person, that I'm drawn to others' struggles?' He almost recoiled. 'I must see this through.'

In her mind, she was transported back to a train station nearly thirteen years earlier. She could see herself at eight years old, sitting happily beside her mother, ice cream cone in hand, oblivious to the tragedy about to unfold. The memory was so vivid she could almost taste the vanilla, feel the sticky sweetness on her fingers as she watched her mother stand and walk toward the train tracks.

The approaching train's rumble grew louder in her memory, matching the accelerating rhythm of her heart. Her mother waited by the edge as the train screamed toward them, and Lucy's childhood innocence shattered in that moment—the moment she screamed in horror as the train collided with her mother's body.

Chaos erupted around her young self, but all she could recall now was the raw emotion etched on her own face—horror and confusion that would never fully leave her.

"I thought losing her would bring me and my dad closer," Lucy continued, her expression distant as she spoke.

The years after her mother's suicide played through her mind like a fragmented film reel—interactions with her father at various ages, each scene showing increasing disconnection. At eight, her tearful attempts to reach him met with awkward, inadequate comfort. At ten, her efforts to engage him in conversation during dinner receiving only monosyllabic responses. By twelve, their interactions had become purely functional, and by sixteen, the emotional numbing in her father had created a wall she no longer tried to scale.

"But it drove a wedge between us," she told Peter, sadness weighing her words.

Each stage of her childhood showed her longing for connection, only to be met with her father's coldness—his inability to process his own grief creating a void where their relationship should have been.

"Even though I resented him... I understood," Lucy admitted, her face showing the complex emotions attached to the memory. "I felt empty too."

As she spoke, images from her own life flashed through her mind: nights spent seeking oblivion through drugs, meaningless sexual encounters with strangers whose names she never learned, moments of despair that led her to destructive behaviours.

Her teenage years had been a desperate attempt to feel something—anything—to fill the numbness that had become her constant companion. She recalled snorting cocaine in grimy bathrooms, engaging in casual, emotionless sex, trying frantically to escape the void inside her.

"I just wanted to feel something... anything," she explained, her voice barely above a whisper. "But I was always met with nothingness."

Peter reached out, impulsively, to take her hand. He immediately regretted it. 'Too much, too soon. She'll think I'm clingy.' But then she squeezed his hand back, her eyes meeting his with a look of gratitude. 'Maybe she needs this as much as I do.' He didn't release her hand.

The memories of self-harm surfaced next—the sharp edge of a razor against her pale skin, the momentary relief as physical pain temporarily drowned out the emotional numbness, leaving her hollow-eyed and exhausted.

"The irony is..." Lucy paused, gathering her courage to continue. "After years of feeling nothing, the intense feelings that came when the psychosis hit this year... I just couldn't handle it."

Peter remained silent, but his eyes revealed a deep empathy that spoke louder than words could have. The moment hung between them, heavy with vulnerability as Lucy allowed herself to be truly seen, perhaps for the first time.

CHAPTER 9:
TWO WEEKS AGO

Two weeks before their intimate morning and the police officer's visit, Lucy sat on the edge of her bed, anxiety etched into every line of her face. Soft natural light filtered through the curtains, casting stripes across her features that highlighted the tension in her expression. Her phone rested on her lap, anxiously tapped between her fingers as her brow furrowed in thought.

The atmosphere in the room was thick with her inner turmoil, her mind racing with questions and doubts as she contemplated reaching out to Peter—the stranger from the dating app who had somehow become her lifeline in the chaos of her existence.

'How do I even ask him?' she wondered, fear gripping her heart. 'What if he thinks I'm a mess? What if he sees I'm not okay?'

Her hands shook as she twirled the phone between her fingers, indecision paralyzing her. Just as she gathered her courage, Jim's voice cut in, mocking as ever.

'Why not just say, Hey, I'm a complete lunatic who battered a tramp to death with a brick'? That'll go over well!'

Lucy flinched at the intrusion, biting her lip as she tried to drown out the noise. She stood and began pacing the room, attempting to calm her racing heart and quiet the voices that continued to plague her, even after her initial meeting with Peter.

'No, it has to be normal,' she told herself, anxiety coursing through her veins. 'Just casual. Not too clingy.

Just... ask him if he wants to disconnect from reality and come to my mad-house.'

She stopped abruptly, her breath catching as she brought up her texting app. She typed slowly, the cursor blinking in rhythm with her accelerated heartbeat.

"Hey Peter, how have you been?" she typed, then immediately deleted the words. "No, too formal..." she muttered.

She tried again: "Hey! I just finished cleaning—" but stopped, looking around her chaotic room filled with remnants of her struggles. Doubt replaced the timid smile that had briefly appeared on her face as Jim's voice returned, dripping with sarcasm.

'Cleaning? You can't even clean your mind!'

Lucy took a deep breath, shaking her head to banish Jim's taunts, and continued typing—only to delete her words again, dissatisfied with every attempt.

'What if he thinks I'm crazy?' The thought raced through her mind, sending a fresh wave of anxiety through her. 'What if he sees all the mess and... And me?'

She gripped her hair in frustration, resuming her pacing across the worn carpet.

"Peter, want to come over?" she typed, then immediately backspaced the words. "No, that sounds needy!"

She tried again: "Maybe… a coffee? If you're free…" but deleted that too.

"Ugh, forget this," she muttered, throwing the phone onto the bed in a moment of despair. It bounced against the mattress and landed face-up, the screen illuminating with a new notification—a message from Peter.

"Hey Lucy, everything okay? I'm here if you want to talk."

Her heart raced, a mixture of relief and terror flooding her system. She stood frozen, battling the voices in her head once more.

'You can't even have a conversation without sounding like a total idiot', she chastised herself, the self-deprecation almost comforting in its familiarity.

Jim's voice burst in, almost sing-song in its mockery: 'Maybe just say, 'I'm fine, just a bit of a lunatic over here! Want to join the life of chaos?'

Despite herself, Lucy smirked, shaking her head at her mind's cruel humour. Then, summoning her courage, she took a deep breath and opened a new message, her fingers typing tentatively.

"Hey, would you like to come over today? Kind of looking for company... ;)"

She hesitated over the send button, her heart racing with apprehension and hope mingled together. After what seemed like an eternity, she pressed SEND, letting the moment linger, filled with uncertainty about what might follow.

Lucy stood nervously by the window, arms wrapped tightly around her waist as if holding herself together. She peered through the thin curtains, watching the street below with anxious eyes. Though sunlight flooded the pavement outside, it felt distant to her, almost ominous, as the familiar voices began bubbling beneath the surface of her consciousness.

'What if he says no?' She thought, her stomach knotting with anxiety. 'What if he thinks I'm a freak?'

Her reflection in the window glass showed the anxiety flickering across her features—the tension in her jaw, the slight furrow of her brow, the way her eyes darted to check each passing figure on the street below.

'You can't leave,' the voices whispered, growing in strength and number. 'What if they see you? He'll see the real you, the broken you. What if there's a police car outside when you walk out?'

She bit her lip until she nearly drew blood, feeling panic flood back through her veins. With a deep breath, she stepped away from the window, frustration boiling to the surface as she checked her phone again for a reply, finding nothing.

"Come on, Peter," she whispered to herself, her voice barely audible in the quiet apartment.

Minutes stretched into what felt like hours as Lucy stood with the phone gripped tightly in her hand, her heart aching with both hope and fear. The ambient sounds of the street outside—cars passing, distant voices, and the occasional slamming door—blended with the turmoil inside her head, creating a discordant symphony that threatened to overwhelm her.

Lucy's fingers nervously drummed against her leg as her eyes darted repeatedly toward her phone on the table. The atmosphere in the apartment grew heavy with anticipation, her heart racing while she fought against the rising tide of anxiety.

'What if he doesn't want to come?' The thought circled in her mind, relentless and cruel. 'What if he thinks I'm a freak?'

Across town, Peter lounged on his couch, staring at his phone with an intensity that belied his casual posture. He bit his lip, a mixture of excitement and apprehension etched across his face. The silence in his apartment felt suffocating loud, broken only by the ticking of a clock and the occasional car horn from the street below.

"Okay, stay calm," he muttered to himself, running a hand through his dishevelled hair. "Just hang out... No big deal."

But it was a big deal, and they both knew it. This wasn't just another hookup from the dating app. Something about Lucy had gotten under his skin from their first messages—a vulnerability that resonated with his own hidden brokenness, a connection he hadn't expected to find.

Back in Lucy's apartment, she grabbed her phone once more, refreshing the screen to check for a reply that wasn't there. Her fingers trembled as the voices started echoing inside her head again, louder and more insistent.

'He better be happy to come over', they taunted mercilessly. 'You can't go out in public anymore. The police are out to get you!'

Lucy gripped her head, fingers digging into her scalp as she tried to drown out the relentless noise, but it only grew louder. The light in her apartment seemed to dim around her, and she felt the very air shifting, transforming into something else entirely.

Suddenly, the scene around her warped—her familiar living room disappeared, replaced by an eerie, abandoned prison. Dusty sunlight filtered through high barred windows; cobwebs draped across the corners of the room. The prison atmosphere felt heavy, oppressive, closing in around her with each passing second.

The once familiar surroundings of her home now felt alien and suffocating, twisted by her mind into a manifestation of her deepest fears. The Prison Guard appeared again before her, broad-shouldered and imposing in his uniform. He banged his truncheon against the wall rhythmically, creating a menacing clatter that reverberated through the cell.

'No! Get away from me! This isn't real!' She screamed internally; her body frozen in place.

The guard's laughter mixed with the relentless cacophony of voices that echoed around her, bouncing off the stone walls of her imaginary prison.

'You belong here,' they whispered in unison. 'They won't let you out. You think you can escape?'

Lucy stumbled backward, her heart racing as she gripped her phone tightly, the plastic case digging into her palm. She was trapped in her own psyche, shadows of torment looming ever closer, threatening to consume her entirely.

In his apartment, Peter had begun pacing nervously around his living room, phone in hand. Anxiety rippled beneath his calm exterior as he glanced repeatedly at the screen, desperately willing it to light up with a reply from Lucy.

'What if she's just looking for a friend,' he thought, self-doubt creeping in? 'She's cute, how can I just be my normal self? Fuck, why do I need this validation, what the fuck is wrong with me?'

He took a deep breath, fingers hovering over the screen, feeling the pressure of his thoughts surging like an untamed tide. Despite his outward appearance of confidence, these moments of waiting stripped away his carefully constructed facade, revealing the insecurities that plagued him daily.

In Lucy's mind, the prison cell grew smaller, the walls closing in around her. She felt the grip of the imaginary space tightening around her chest, making it difficult to breathe. The guard stepped closer, expertly wielding his truncheon as he leered at her.

"You think they'll believe you?" he boomed, his voice echoing off the stone walls. "Look at you! You're a lost cause!"

The voices crescendo, drowning her in a torrent of despair, mocking her very existence with their cruel taunts.

'You made this prison,' they reminded her. 'You can't escape!'

Lucy screamed, the sound echoing through the hollow prison walls of her flat. She shook her head violently, desperately trying to retreat into the recesses of her mind, fighting against the panic rising within her.

Back in reality, Peter finally steeled his nerves. He took a decisive breath and started typing a response to Lucy's message, his thumb hovering briefly over the send button before committing.

"Love to ;)"

Simple, casual, yet containing a promise that made his heart race. He hit send and waited, unaware of the battle being waged in Lucy's mind at that very moment.

Lucy's eyes widened suddenly as she was yanked back to the present, the illusion of the prison dissipating like morning mist. The ambient noise quieted, leaving her breathless, heart pounding against her ribs. She stood in her living room once more, the familiar surroundings a blessed relief after the nightmare landscape of her hallucination.

Her phone lit up in her hand, the screen glowing vibrantly, illuminating the darkness of her thoughts. She hesitated, a mixture of hope and dread coursing through her as she unlocked the device.

"Love to ;)"

Slowly, a smile broke through her distress, warmth spreading through her chest. For a fleeting moment, hope glimmered through the cracks of her despair, pushing back the shadows that constantly threatened to engulf her. But the echoes of her hallucination lingered at the edges of her consciousness, threatening to pull her back into chaos at any moment.

She took a deep breath, battling her inner demons as she prepared for whatever might come next. The weight of silence hung heavy in the apartment as she stood there, phone clutched to her chest, treading the fragile line between hope and despair that had become her daily existence.

Chapter 10:
The Weight of Confession

"What was that about? Why was there a policeman looking for you?"

Peter's question hung in the air between them, shattering the brief happiness they had found in each other's arms. Lucy's face froze, anxiety washing over her features like a wave. She felt the walls closing in, her carefully constructed façade crumbling under the weight of reality.

Without warning, she broke down, tears streaming down her cheeks as the truth she had been trying to hide from herself and the world came spilling out.

"It's the police... they're investigating me," she sobbed, her voice breaking. "I didn't know what was happening. I panicked... I attacked a homeless man. I can't tell what's real anymore!"

The words hung in the air between them, heavy with implications. Lucy's expression turned vacant and emotionless as her paranoia gripped her tightly once more, threatening to drag her back into the abyss.

Peter's brow furrowed as he processed her words, deep in thought about what to do next. His silence scared her more than any reaction she had anticipated. In that moment of vulnerability, with her darkest secret laid bare, Lucy felt more exposed than she had ever been.

As Peter contemplated his response, his mind drifted to his own past—moments that had shaped him, wounds that had never fully healed.

He saw himself in fragments - a child walking school corridors alone, peers' whispers following in his wake. The awkwardness of youth had morphed into teenage isolation, creating barriers between him and the world he desperately wanted to join. The pattern continued through the years - rejection played out across bars and clubs, connections evaporating as quickly as they formed. Eventually dating apps provided temporary escape, although these provided a new form of trauma. These stretched from fabricated pregnancies; to cheating partners; to producing fake online accounts in his name. The experiences shaped him, teaching harsh lessons about trust and human nature.

'Eventually, intense relationships that always ended in rejection started to fade away,' Peter reflected. 'They were replaced by a calmness, a clear inevitability.'

The mood of his memories shifted, revealing the emotional detachment he had cultivated despite his deep-seated fear of solitude. He had learned to expect little, to invest less, to protect the fragile parts of himself that had been broken too many times.

Peter developed an emotional detachment whereby he viewed women as a necessary but disposal object, temporary escapes from the emptiness inside.

His recent pattern had become predictable—hosting a woman for dinner, sharing an Indian curry and rosé wine, enjoying a casual evening while watching something on TV. Lines of some illicit substance might appear on the table, lowering inhibitions, blurring the edges of loneliness. They would have sex, the atmosphere casual, yet Peter's expression would reveal a sense of emptiness, the women entirely replaceable in his emotional landscape.

But with Lucy, it feels different, he realized as his thoughts returned to the present moment. It feels more real than it has for a long time. Maybe it's because she's as messed up as I am. Or maybe it's because she's the first person who's ever really seen me, all my flaws and all my baggage, and hasn't run away screaming. Or does it? Is the difference with Lucy that the inevitability of abandonment isn't there because she is so messed up, that she needs me? Is this difference in dynamic drastically altering my perception of how I feel? Whatever it is, I can't let her go.

Peter took a steadying breath, his brow still furrowed in concern as he looked at Lucy's tear-streaked face. The atmosphere was thick with tension, with possibility, with fear.

'What am I doing?' Peter wondered, staring at Lucy's tear-streaked face. 'I barely know this woman. Why am I even considering throwing my life away for her? What is wrong with me?' Peter often mused that nothing truly mattered, that life was a meaningless flicker between two eternities of darkness. Yet, the illogical spark of connection he felt with Lucy defied this bleak philosophy, a nagging whisper that perhaps, just perhaps, there was something worth saving—even if it destroyed him in the process. He was aware that his longing to be wanted and needed would eventually be his downfall.

'It's not about saving her, or being a hero. It's about not being alone. It's about clinging to something, anything, to avoid facing the emptiness. I know this is probably a disaster waiting to happen, that she's probably going to drag me down with her, but I'm too much of a coward to walk away. Why do I cling to women like this, what the fuck is wrong with me?'

"Lucy... listen to me," he said gently.

She looked up, her face reflecting a complex mixture of fear and vulnerability. Peter knelt beside the bed, his voice soft yet resolute as he made a decision that would alter both their paths.

"I don't care what the police say. I'm here for you. But we need to come up with a plan."

As he spoke, a darker thought crossed his mind. 'If she's on the run, she'll need me. She won't leave.' He hated himself for thinking it, for trying to manipulate her vulnerability. But the need to be needed, to be valued, was a powerful drug. He quickly pushed the thought aside. 'I'm doing this because I care about her. That's all.'

Lucy's eyes widened, confusion battling with sorrow as she shook her head, struggling to process the gravity of the situation.

"A plan? What are you talking about? I can't just run away!" she exclaimed breathlessly.

Though Peter's expression remained that of a compassionate lover, internally his thoughts revealed a deeper, more complex motivation. A deep insecurity and a willingness to leverage the situation to his advantage unfolded in his mind.

'As fucked up as this situation may be,' he thought privately, 'as long as she needs me, she won't leave.'

He watched as Lucy glanced at the wall, her mind clearly racing through possibilities and consequences. For her, the idea of escape brought both terror and a strange allure.

'What if... running away is the only way to escape?' She wondered silently. 'But the thought terrifies me.'

Peter noticed her hesitation and continued, urgency building in his voice as he laid out the possibility of escape, framing it with hope rather than desperation.

"We could go off the grid. Get away from everything and everyone... even the police," he suggested, warming to the idea as he spoke. "You can change your appearance—dye your hair, maybe even find a new name."

As he spoke, Peter's mind raced, envisioning a life far removed from his current existence. A life of adventure, of freedom, of being truly alive for the first time. It was a reckless fantasy, but one he couldn't resist.

His conviction shone through, pulling at Lucy's troubled core. The desperation in her eyes began to transform into a cautious intrigue as she considered his words.

'What would that be like?' She wondered. 'To just... disappear?'

"And I'll help you through the psychosis," Peter continued earnestly. "We can get you some Olanzapine — it's effective. You can't go through the NHS. They'd find you in a heartbeat if you're on their radar."

A pulse of fear charged the air between them, but something else was emerging as well—a sense of possibility, of freedom. Lucy's thoughts remained conflicted, torn between hope and suspicion.

'He cares for me like no one else,' she thought. 'Maybe we could run... But what if this is just another escape that won't fix anything?'

With newfound conviction, Peter gently took her hand, their fingers interlocking—a symbol of their bond, a pact against the world that had hurt them both.

"We won't have to run far," he said softly. "Just far enough to breathe and figure things out together."

A moment of silence hung between them, charged with unspoken fears and possibilities. Lucy's eyes searched his face, feeling more connected than ever in their shared vulnerability.

He squeezed her hand again, offering a reassuring smile. But inside, he felt a tremor of fear. He was committing to something huge, something dangerous. 'What if this all goes wrong? What if I can't protect her?' He pushed the doubt aside. 'I can't back out now, I've just offered my help and support. Besides, a life on the run… that could be interesting.'

"You really believe we can do that?" she asked, her voice trembling with uncertainty.

Peter nodded earnestly, squeezing her hand gently, providing a sense of certainty amidst her turmoil. "I promise you, Lucy. We can figure it out. Just the two of us."

Lucy hesitated, vulnerability battling with the flicker of hope his words had kindled. She swallowed hard, her logical mind grappling with the emotional sanctuary Peter offered.

'As long as I have him,' she thought, 'I won't have to face this alone. Maybe I can breathe again.'

Peter brought out a small duffel bag from the closet, signalling action amidst the emotional haze. He began searching through it, his movements purposeful.

"First, we should pack some essentials—clothes you won't be recognized in, anything that could help you blend in."

Lucy watched him, lost in thought as a whirlwind of emotions swept through her—a mix of excitement and trepidation. She rose from the bed, drawn into the momentum he created.

"Okay... but what if someone sees us?" she asked, her voice steadier than before.

"We'll figure it out," Peter assured her. "I know some spots where we can lay low until its safe."

Lucy pushed aside her trepidation, feeling a flicker of hope ignite within her fragmented spirit. 'This could be my chance,' she whispered to herself.

As they began to pack together, the mood shifted from despair to a cautious sense of camaraderie. Each item they placed in the bag symbolized a step toward liberation—an escape from the darkness that loomed over them.

"We might even find a beach," Peter suggested with a half-smile. "Just you and me, away from everything."

Lucy smiled faintly, the idea lifting her spirits just a bit, even as shadows lingered around them. Their connection deepened with every item packed as they prepared to face the unknown together, bound by their shared brokenness and the desperate hope that they might somehow heal each other.

Chapter 11:
The Favor

Peter stood outside Lucy's apartment building, his brow furrowed with determination. He glanced back up at her window, where she peeked anxiously through the curtain, waiting for his return. With a steadying breath, he resolved to do what needed to be done—to help this woman who had somehow become essential to him in such a short time.

He knew this was a risk, that asking Graham for help could have serious consequences. But he was desperate, and he couldn't bear the thought of Lucy suffering because of his inaction. 'I have to do this for her', he thought, steeling his nerves. 'I can't let her down'.

"Alright, let's get this sorted," he muttered to himself before getting into his car.

Minutes later, Peter pulled up to a quaint suburban house, the sun casting a warm glow over the well-kept garden. This was familiar territory—Graham's house, a place he had visited many times before. He parked at the curb, took one last deep breath to centre himself, and stepped out of the car, determination etched on his face.

Peter stood by the front door for a long moment, not moving. The silence in the air pressed all around him, sticky and suffocating, amplifying the chaos in his head. He stared at his reflection in the window—tousled hair, bloodshot eyes, the face of a man who should know better. 'What the fuck am I doing?' The question came out of nowhere and echoed through his skull. 'Why am I about to risk everything for a woman I barely know?' He tried to tell himself it was love, but he couldn't even say the word in his own mind without cringing. Was it even possible to love someone this quickly, someone this broken? Or was it something else? Something uglier and more desperate. Some need to be needed, to matter to someone, even if that someone was a car crash in slow motion. He pressed his forehead to the cold glass, fighting the urge to scream.

'Why am I so damaged that I'm putting myself in danger for a girl who might be as dangerous as she is vulnerable?'

He thought about all those women before: the ones who'd smiled politely and drifted away, the ones who'd stuck around just long enough to get bored, the ones who'd left him feeling emptier than before. Maybe that's the real problem, he thought. Maybe the carousel of shallow connections, the endless cycle of dinner, sex, and ghosting, is safer than this. Safer than trying to play hero with a bottle of pills you know nothing about, for a woman you can't save, with no clue what the right dose even is. One wrong move, and she ends up sicker—or worse. But he couldn't stop himself. He couldn't make himself walk away. What did that say about him? That this was the only way he knew how to feel alive—to be wanted, to be useful, to be necessary, if only for a moment? He squeezed his eyes shut. "You're pathetic," he whispered to his reflection. "You'll do it anyway." And he would. Because the alternative—being alone, being nothing to no one—was unthinkable. With a deep, unsteady breath, Peter turned away from the window and finally stepped out into the cold, keys jangling in his fist. Whatever happened next, he'd have to live with it. Or not.

At the front door, Peter rang the doorbell, hands fidgeting in his pockets as he waited. His mind raced with possible approaches, ways to frame his request without revealing too much. After a moment that seemed to stretch forever, the door swung open, revealing Julia—Graham's mother, a woman in her sixties with a warm manner but slightly frazzled appearance. She greeted him with a genuine smile that made him feel momentarily guilty about his true purpose for visiting.

"Peter! It's so good to see you. Come in!" she exclaimed, stepping aside to let him enter.

Peter nodded appreciatively as he stepped into the familiar home, the scent of freshly baked cookies hanging in the air. Julia led him through to the kitchen, a bright and homey space where Graham sat at the table, scrolling through his phone. At twenty-five, Graham looked dishevelled as always, but Peter knew his appearance belied a sharp wit and intelligence.

Graham looked up as Peter entered, surprise and pleasure crossing his features. "Hey, mate! What brings you here?"

They exchanged casual pleasantries, falling into the rhythm of familiarity that came from years of friendship. Julia excused herself to another room, leaving the two men alone. As soon as she was out of earshot, Peter's expression shifted, becoming more serious.

"I actually need a favour," he said, his voice hesitant but direct.

Graham looked curious, putting his phone down and giving Peter his full attention. The gesture both encouraged and unsettled Peter—Graham had always been perceptive, able to read between the lines of what people said.

"There's this girl..." Peter began, choosing his words carefully. "She's been... struggling. Psychosis, episodes... It's rough. I need to get her some olanzapine to help stabilize her until she can see a doctor."

A brief silence followed his request, the only sound in the room coming from the ticking of the wall clock.

Graham's brow furrowed in thought, but Peter could see the scepticism in his eyes, the questions forming.

"Olanzapine, huh?" Graham said finally. "Sounds serious. Why not just tell her to get a prescription?"

"It's a lot more complicated than that," Peter replied, urgency creeping into his voice. "She's scared and needs something now. I wouldn't ask if I didn't think it was necessary."

Graham studied Peter's face, seeming to weigh the sincerity of his concern against the strangeness of the request. Peter held his gaze, allowing his genuine worry for Lucy to show.

"You know I don't take my meds, right?" Graham said after a long moment.

Peter nodded, understanding the implication. Graham had been prescribed various medications over the years but had developed a complicated relationship with them, often choosing to manage his own condition through other means.

"I know," Peter acknowledged, "but this is different. I care about her; I want to help her."

Graham hesitated, visibly weighing his options. With a reluctant sigh, he reached into a cabinet above the sink, pulling out a beautifully kept wooden box that Peter had never seen before.

"Here... take it," Graham said, passing the box to Peter. "Just this once."

Peter's eyes widened in disbelief as he accepted the box, glancing down at the label. Inside was a full month's supply of olanzapine, untouched and perfectly preserved.

"Gra—this is a month's worth!" Peter exclaimed, shocked by his friend's generosity.

Graham shrugged, a hint of defiance in his posture. "Yeah, well, I haven't had an episode in ages. And I barely use them anyway. Just do me a favour and make sure she actually takes them. I don't want to feel like I'm enabling something… you know?"

Peter took a moment to absorb the unexpected generosity, the weight of the box in his hands matched by the weight of responsibility he felt. He placed a hand on Graham's shoulder, gratitude mixing with the burden he carried for Lucy's sake.

"I promise I will," Peter said earnestly. "Thank you, Graham. This means a lot."

With a nod, Peter turned to leave, the box of medication a tangible reminder of the path he had chosen— a path of deception and flight, but also one of protection and care. As he stepped back into the sunlight, determination rose in his chest. He had what they needed now; they could move forward with their plan.

As he walked back to his car, Peter's thoughts drifted to Graham. He knew his friend had his own demons, his own struggles with mental illness. He hoped he wasn't burdening him too much, that his request wouldn't trigger a relapse. Why was Peter risking his friend's welfare for a girl he barely knew? Peter wondered what was wrong with him, questioning both the morality and sanity of his decisions. Is his new-found love for Lucy down to a yearning for a meaning and connection in his life?

He walked back to his car, the medication secure in his pocket, thoughts of Lucy filling his mind. For better or worse, their fates were now intertwined. There would be no turning back.

As Peter headed toward his car, he glanced back at Graham, who stood in the doorway, a look of concern etched on his face.

"Just keep an eye on her, alright?" Graham called out, the worry in his voice unmistakable.

Peter raised the box slightly in a gesture of acknowledgment before getting into his car. The atmosphere was thick with looming uncertainty, yet somehow tinged with a sense of hope—the possibility that he might actually be able to help Lucy in a way no one else could.

As Peter drove back to Lucy, he couldn't shake the feeling that he was being used. Graham's words echoed in his mind - 'Just keep an eye on her, alright?' "What does he know that I don't? Does everyone see me as some kind of pathetic caretaker?" he wondered, gripping the steering wheel tightly.

He glanced at the box of medication on the passenger seat, a wave of resentment washing over him. "She better be worth it," he muttered, his voice laced with bitterness. "I'm risking everything for her, and if this all goes to shit, I swear..." He trailed off, unable to articulate the full extent of his anger and frustration. All he knew was that he was teetering on the edge of something dangerous, and he wasn't sure if he was strong enough to pull back.

Peter gripped the steering wheel tightly, conflicted emotions swirling within him as he prepared to drive back to Lucy. The stakes had never felt higher. He had crossed a line, obtaining prescription medication under false pretences, committing himself to a plan that would likely involve running from the authorities. Yet as he drove, echoes of Lucy's vulnerability played in his mind, strengthening his resolve. For once in his life, someone needed him—truly needed him—and he wouldn't let her down.

Chapter 12:
The World Outside

While Peter was obtaining the medication, Lucy sat curled up on her sofa, blankly watching the news as it flickered on the television. The muted sounds of various reports blended into a cacophony of discontent, reflecting the chaos inside her own mind. Her living room remained cluttered, remnants of her fractured life scattered around like physical manifestations of her mental state.

On the screen, an anchor-person in their forties delivered the news with practiced urgency, headlines scrolling beneath in an endless ticker of distress.

"Tonight, the nation faces unprecedented unrest as the cost-of-living crisis continues to escalate," the reporter announced. "Families struggle to make ends meet, with inflation driven by the failed North Sea oil project reaching a staggering 10 percent."

Lucy's fingers twitched nervously, her anxiety manifesting in subtle movements as she watched, captivated. Images of families queuing for food banks flashed across the screen, their expressions a mixture of desperation and resilience that resonated with something deep inside her.

"In other news, tensions rise amid the 'Fortress Britain' immigration policies," the anchor-person continued. "The Prime Minister has vowed to 'reclaim our borders,' prompting protests and deepening divisions."

"Reports of xenophobic attacks have surged, with mosques vandalized and immigrant communities feeling increasingly threatened," the news continued relentlessly. "Authorities have launched investigations, yet many feel unsafe in their own neighbourhoods, especially after the White Rose terror attack."

Images of burnt mosques and somber gatherings of community members grieving together filled the screen. Lucy's breath caught in her throat, the weight of the world's injustices pressing down on her already fragile psyche. She turned her gaze downward, her internal turmoil palpable even in the silence of her apartment.

'What is happening to us?' she wondered. 'Are we all just victims of our fears?'

The screen shifted again to families displaced by war, forced to flee their homelands. Lucy leaned forward, her brow furrowing as she observed their expressions. She couldn't shake the uncanny connection she felt with their despair—like fragmented pieces of her own life reflecting back at her through the television glass.

"As communities fracture and voices of dissent rise," the anchor-person intoned, "citizens grapple with their identities, questioning what it means to belong in a country rife with uncertainty." Unbeknownst to most, these struggles became data points in a network extending far beyond London, harvested for purposes few could imagine.

Her phone buzzed beside her, its screen illuminating briefly in the dim room. Lucy glanced at it but didn't pick it up—caught between her digital world and the aching reality unfolding on screen. The news began to fade into a montage of headlines, each more alarming than the last.

'When did we become so... lost?' She whispered to herself, the question hanging unanswered in the quiet apartment.

Tears welled in Lucy's eyes as she watched, the sudden surge of emotions causing her heart to race. She wiped her cheeks, feeling the weight of helplessness—the very essence of being trapped within her thoughts and the troubled world outside. The parallels between her internal chaos and the external world's turmoil weren't lost on her; both seemed equally beyond her control.

The news reports in the background gradually faded from her awareness, leaving only the sound of her racing heart—a reminder of the fight she still had inside her, even if at this moment, it felt overshadowed by the heaviness surrounding her.

With a sudden decision, she turned off the television, plunging the room into quiet. She stared into the empty space before her, struggling with a sense of purpose—a desire to escape her chaos while the world grappled with its own. The juxtaposition of her personal struggles against the broader societal issues loomed overhead like a storm cloud, pressing in on her reality from all sides.

Chapter 13:
The Raid

Night had fallen by the time Lucy began to seriously worry about Peter. She sat cross-legged on the sofa, her eyes flickering nervously between the darkened window and her phone. It had been hours since she had last heard from him, and anxiety gnawed at her with increasing intensity.

'What if I put him in danger...?' The thought formed unbidden, adding to her mounting fear.

As if triggered by her dark thoughts, a loud knock suddenly reverberated through the apartment. Lucy jumped, her heart racing, dread flooding her system like ice water in her veins.

"Peter?" she whispered hopefully, though something in her gut told her it wasn't him.

Silence swelled around her until another knock, louder this time, rattled through the apartment. She scrambled to her feet, glancing at her phone—its screen remained dark, no messages from Peter. She moved quietly toward the door, her footsteps cushioned by the carpet as she peered through the peephole.

Through the distorted glass, she spotted two police officers standing sternly outside, their expressions grim and determined. Her breath caught in her throat as fear gripped her with paralyzing intensity.

Just as the tension built toward what seemed like an inevitable confrontation, Jim appeared in the corner of her vision, his grin sharp and cruel, his eyes alight with malicious pleasure at her predicament.

"Where's lover boy at?" Jim's voice echoed mockingly in her mind. "You thought he'd help you? Just like your mother? Left you behind, just like every other fool in your life."

"Lucy Evans! Open up!" one of the officers shouted through the door. "We need to speak with you!"

Panic spiralled within her, each breath becoming shallower than the last. She stepped back, heart pounding against her ribs, her mind racing through every possible outcome. The voices in her head began to echo once again, growing in volume and intensity with each passing second.

'They know how you feel! They know!' The voices chanted in unison, drowning out rational thought.

In a frantic movement, Lucy dashed around the apartment, looking for any possible escape route. She peeked through the curtain again, spotting the officers whispering to each other; one was reaching into his pocket, likely pulling out something—a weapon? A taser? Her imagination ran wild with possibilities, none of them good.

'I can't get caught!' The thought pounded in her mind with each frantic heartbeat.

Suddenly, she remembered the balcony. With renewed purpose, she veered toward the balcony door, yanking it open with trembling hands, struggling to balance between her resolve and the paralyzing fear that threatened to root her to the spot.

Before she could step outside, another loud knock shook the door, followed by a heavy bang—the officers were trying to break in, the wood splintering around the lock. Moments later, the door frame splintered as a battering ram slammed against it.

The door burst open moments later, and the officers charged inside, their heavy footsteps echoing through the small apartment. Lucy leaped out onto the balcony, heart pounding as she looked down at the alleyway below—it was a steep drop, far enough to cause serious injury if she simply jumped.

"Clear!" one officer called out, his voice echoing from the hallway as they systematically searched the apartment.

Lucy scanned her surroundings, her palms sweaty against the cool metal railing. In the dim light, she spotted a fire escape ladder attached to the side of the building. A burst of adrenaline spiked through her system, giving her a momentary clarity amidst the panic.

With newfound resolve, she hopped onto the fire escape ladder, gripping the metal rungs tightly as she began to descend. Below, the sound of footsteps echoed through the apartment as the officers edged closer to the balcony, their confusion evident in their raised voices.

"Bursting in, Miss Evans! We know you're here!" one officer shouted, his voice carrying through the open balcony door and into the night air.

Lucy continued her descent, ignoring the painful bite of the cold metal against her palms. When she reached the bottom, she dropped low, pulling her legs beneath her as her feet touched the ground. She made sure to stay hidden in the shadows, her breath ragged and visible in the cool night air, adrenaline coursing through her system as she looked back up at her apartment—a place that had once been her sanctuary, now transformed into a trap from which she had narrowly escaped.

"She's gotta be here! Check every corner!" a second officer's voice carried from above, frustration evident in his tone.

Keeping to the shadows, Lucy felt the weight of the world pressing down on her shoulders with crushing force. With quick, decisive movements, she darted off down the alley, adrenaline propelling her away from the chaos behind her. Her mind focused on a single thought: Peter. She needed to find him before it was too late.

Chapter 14:
Shadows and Voices

Lucy navigated through the dimly-lit alley, her heart thudding in her chest as she raced past overflowing trash cans and broken bottles. The ambient sounds of the city—distant traffic, the occasional siren, the hum of air conditioning units—created an eerie soundtrack to her flight. The shadows seemed to morph around her, amplifying her paranoia, but she fought against the creeping desolation that threatened to overwhelm her.

'This isn't the end,' she whispered to herself, a mantra of determination. 'I won't let it be the end!'

With renewed resolve etched into her features, she found an escape route at the end of the alley—a narrow passage between two buildings that led to another street. She could hear the echo of sirens drawing nearer and the muffled shouts of officers searching for her. Pushing herself harder, she disappeared into the shadows, an uncertain future waiting in the darkness ahead.

As Lucy stumbled deeper into the labyrinthine back alleys, the shadows wrapped around her like a suffocating blanket. Her breath came in ragged gasps, and the adrenaline that had carried her this far began to fade, leaving her vulnerable to the thoughts and voices that constantly plagued her.

Suddenly, the murmurs in her head grew loud, drowning out the sounds of the city. Jim's familiar voice cut through the fog of her mind, turning her senses into chaos.

'Oh, look at you, Lucy,' he taunted, his tone dripping with mockery. 'Running scared. You think you actually escaped?'

Lucy staggered, feeling her grasp on reality slip further away. She shook her head violently, trying to dispel the voices, but they only intensified.

"Get away from me!" she cried out, her voice echoing off the brick walls surrounding her. "You're not real!"

A vivid flashback flooded her mind without warning—images swirling like debris in a tornado. She saw Jim pinned above her, his laughter echoing through her bedroom, his features morphing into something monstrous as he grasped her shoulders.

'Remember our little chat?' Jim's voice permeated the memory. 'Karma's a bitch, Lucy. You decided to stab me in the neck, didn't you?'

Back in the alley, Lucy's heart hammered against her ribcage. She clutched her head, digging her fingers into her scalp as she tried to dispel Jim's voice.

"You're a rapist!" she screamed into the empty alley. "You attacked me!"

'None of that really happened, sweetheart,' Jim's voice laughed inside her mind. 'All a figment of that staggering imagination of yours.'

Lucy's face twisted in panic as she questioned the reality around her. Dizziness overcame her, her vision blurring at the edges. The walls of the alley seemed to close in around her, shadows shifting in her peripheral vision, taking on forms that weren't there.

The alley warped and distorted in her perception—graffiti on the walls coming alive, faces of imaginary onlookers twisted in perpetual judgment. She couldn't tell what was real and what wasn't. The interplay of shadows and light drove her deeper into despair with each passing moment.

'Is this real?' she wondered, terror gripping her heart. 'Am I actually seeing them or am I falling apart again?'

'It's all very real, Lucy,' Jim's voice replied, gently mocking but with a hint of sympathy that confused her even more. 'Like the blood on your hands. You can't escape that.'

As Lucy stumbled through the alley, the walls pulsed with colour in her vision, shadows elongating and curling around her feet like serpents. The air seemed to thicken, heavy with the scent of decay, tinged with a metallic sharpness that made her heart race even faster.

Her hands trembled as she touched her flushed cheeks, feeling warmth seep through her fingers—a stark reminder of the night's horrors, of everything she was running from.

Lucy dropped to her knees, fear paralyzing her as she stared into the void ahead. Jim's voice shifted subtly, softening in a way that disturbed her even more than his mockery.

'I'm not your enemy, Lucy,' he said, his tone almost sympathetic. 'I'm here, all the way to the bitter end, remember?'

The chaos around her softened, shadows shifting to provide an illusion of comfort. She squeezed her eyes shut, fighting the deeper pull of despair that threatened to consume her entirely.

"But you're not real," she choked out, tears streaming down her face. "None of this is real."

'I may not be,' Jim conceded, his voice gentler than before, 'but your pain is valid. It's okay to feel lost...'

Lucy's breath steadied slightly, a flicker of sanity battling against the mania that had overtaken her. She inhaled deeply, feeling the warmth of the fleeting connection with Jim—a strange comfort in the midst of her breakdown.

An overwhelming wave of calm suddenly washed over her, though she couldn't identify its source. Lucy pushed herself to her feet, stumbling toward the alley's end, half-aware of her surroundings. Still in a daze, she turned back, taking one last look at the shadows that represented her chaotic reality before stepping into the unknown.

As she emerged onto the dimly lit street, a vehicle suddenly pulled up beside her. Before she could react, she was grabbed from behind and pulled into the car. A small gasp escaped her lips as the door slammed shut behind her.

"What are you doing here?" Peter's voice cut through her confusion, urgent and concerned. "You shouldn't be outside!"

Lucy blinked, still half-immersed in her conversation with Jim. The car interior felt compact, suffocating—a temporary safe haven, yet terrifyingly confining. She pressed herself against the door, unsure if this new development was real.

Peter caught sight of her fear, but relief flooded his face as he reached out to touch her arm gently, confirming his physical presence.

"I was worried about you," he said, his voice softening. "I'm just glad you're safe."

Peter knew his obsession with Lucy defied all logic. He understood, with chilling clarity, that his self-destructive tendencies were rooted in a desperate desire for validation. He, a man who saw the world as a meaningless void, was now willing to risk everything for a woman he barely knew, a woman who was clearly spiralling out of control. He saw the trap Lucy presented, the inevitable pain that awaited him at the end of this path. It was irrational, reckless, and utterly doomed. And yet, he couldn't stop himself. It was like an itch he was compelled to scratch, even if it meant tearing his own skin raw. As Lucy sat in the backseat, the allure of reality blurred again. She remained tangled in her psychosis, everything around her feeling surreal and distant. The shadows crept back into the edges of her vision, casting doubt even as Peter's comforting presence lingered before her.

'So he found you, huh?' Jim's voice mocked from the empty seat beside her. 'But how did he know? You told him about the police?'

Lucy remained silent, her gaze distant as she wrestled with her faltering reality, voices still swirling around her like leaves in a whirlwind.

'He saved you this time,' Jim continued to press, 'but keep an eye on him. Is he really someone you can trust?'

Overwhelmed by Jim's words, Lucy zoned out from Peter's concerned questions, lost in the battlefield of her mind. The world around her faded as her internal conflict reignited—a battle between her perceived reality and the tenuous promise of safety that Peter represented.

The car drove into the night, Lucy's face a portrait of turmoil, even as her heart yearned for peace—a peace that remained just out of reach, tethered by the tumult of her fractured mind. In the back of the car, a moment of clarity briefly interrupted her paranoia Lucy hinted of a few obscure locations far from any major city. "There are a couple of dodgy B&Bs I know of," she said. "Places people don't usually go looking for things."

Chapter 15:
Confrontations

The dingy corridor of the cheap bed and breakfast was barely lit, revealing stained carpets and peeling wallpaper that spoke of years of neglect. The air smelled of stale cigarettes and cheap disinfectant, creating a grimy, oppressive atmosphere that only enhanced Lucy's sense of unease.

She stood near the reception desk, scanning her surroundings with a mixture of confusion and dread. The sounds of distant thumping muffled through the thin walls amplified her sense of claustrophobia. This place was a far cry from her apartment, but at least it was somewhere to hide—for now.

Peter emerged from the nearby room, a hint of discomfort evident in his posture. He fumbled with the keycard in his pocket as he approached Lucy, unaware of the storm brewing inside her.

"How did you know where to find me, Peter?" Lucy asked, her voice tight and confrontational.

Peter looked taken aback, surprise flickering across his features. "What do you mean? I was just driving around looking for you..."

The tension in the air thickened, suffused with a mixture of anger and suspicion. Lucy's eyes narrowed as she stepped closer, her voice low but fierce. "You didn't just happen to find me! How did you really know?"

Peter shifted uncomfortably, visibly struggling to manage the rising tide of emotions. He swallowed hard, casting his gaze downward before meeting her eyes again.

"Lucy, you should be more appreciative of everything I'm doing!" he snapped, frustration evident in his tone. "This place is gross, but I didn't want you out there alone! You think I'm putting myself at risk for fun?"

Lucy's expression hardened, the voices in her mind growing louder, egging her on to confront him further.

'Push him, Lucy! Don't let him walk all over you!' they urged in unison.

She shuddered, the weight of the voices intertwining with her resolve to seek the truth. Her determination mounted, and Peter could sense the shift in her demeanour.

"Appreciative?" Lucy shot back, her voice rising. "You have no idea! What if this was a ruse? I don't even know who you are anymore."

Peter stiffened, his body language betraying a simmering rage beneath a mask of forced calm. He folded his arms across his chest, clenching his jaw tightly.

"You should be thanking me instead of berating me for trying to help," he said through gritted teeth. "If you think you know what's dangerous…"

Lucy moved closer, invading his personal space, her eyes blazing with intensity. "So, how did you actually find me then?"

Peter's frustration reached a boiling point, and he finally relented, eyes flashing with anger. "I told you! I was just driving past! I saw you talking to yourself in that alleyway!"

Lucy recoiled, disbelief washing over her features. The admission struck her like a physical blow—he had seen her at her most vulnerable, conversing with voices only she could hear.

"That's bullshit, Peter!" she cried, humiliation fuelling her rage.

Without thinking, acting purely on instinct, she delivered a quick punch to Peter's face. The impact sent him stumbling backward, blood spilling from his lip where her knuckles had connected.

"You get ONE of those... ONE!" Peter snarled, rage igniting in his eyes.

He glanced around wildly, letting his anger boil over. In a fit of rage, he picked up a nearby lamp and hurled it across the room. It smashed against the wall, sending ceramic shards flying in all directions. The sound of breaking glass punctuated the tense silence that followed.

Peter's breathing was heavy, his chest rising and falling rapidly as he stormed toward the door, frustration palpable in the air around him.

"I need to get out of here!" he shouted, voice echoing off the thin walls.

He slammed the door behind him, the sound reverberating ominously through the hallway as he stormed out into the night, leaving Lucy alone with her thoughts and fears.

In the sudden silence, Lucy stood frozen, her fists still clenched, a mixture of fear and adrenaline coursing through her veins. She turned her gaze to the bedside table where a small vial of pills sat—the medication Peter had somehow obtained for her earlier. The voices rose immediately, creating a tumult of conflict in her mind.

'Don't do it! You need to stay strong!' They warned.

'You can't let him control you. You need me!' Jim's voice stood out from the others, more insistent, more persuasive.

Feeling lost and overwhelmed yet desperate to regain some sense of control, Lucy held her head in her hands, fingers digging into her scalp.

"I can't... I can't give in to this," she whispered, battling with herself.

In a display of sheer determination, she leaned forward and picked up the vial of pills, her decision crystallizing with each passing second. Drawing in a deep breath, she steadied herself, trying to ignore the chorus of protests from the voices.

"Okay... just take the antipsychotics," she said calmly to herself. "It'll help you think clearly."

With focus, she uncapped the vial and retrieved her first pill, examining it briefly before swallowing it without water. The weight of her choice hung in the quiet room, punctuated only by the distant sound of the city outside and the fading shouts of her inner demons.

The camera of her mind lingered on her own reflection in the cracked mirror on the wall, where the struggle for clarity against the storm of mental chaos played out in slow motion—the faintest glimmer of hope shining through the darkness of her psyche for the first time in what felt like forever.

Chapter 16:
Echoes of the Mind

Jim was not merely a figment of Lucy's imagination, but a haunting figure conjured from the remnants of her shattered past. He existed as a manifestation of the pain and regret that lingered within her fractured psyche, taking form from the darkest corners of her consciousness.

Born from unresolved trauma, Jim thrived in the shadows of her memory, a reminder of the belittling voices that had once drowned out her own. With every mocking laugh, he churned the bitterness of a mother lost and a father distant, feeding the self-loathing that festered in Lucy's heart like an open wound that refused to heal.

As his presence grew more insistent in her mind, the sharpness of his features emphasized his role as tormentor. He embodied all the emotional struggles Lucy faced—each taunt reflecting a wound that stubbornly remained raw and painful, regardless of time's passage.

He was the distortion of her reality, twisting her thoughts into a chaotic tempest that left her feeling lost and alone. In moments of despair, he amplified the darkness, whispering lies that gnawed at her sanity. His laughter echoed her deepest insecurities, suffocating her hopes for liberation from the prison of her mind.

Lucy's tumultuous past—images of loneliness, drug use, and failed relationships—had created fertile ground for Jim's formation. The narrative of her life wove between present struggles and echoes of past traumas, each painful memory strengthening his hold on her consciousness.

Yet Jim was not simply an enemy; he was a reflection of her unfinished grief, an entity engraved with memories she could not escape. Behind his biting mockery lay a yearning for connection—to expose the vulnerability she'd rather hide from the world and herself.

As Lucy grappled with these demons, the lines between reality and delusion blurred ever further. Each confrontation with Jim became a step deeper into the labyrinth of her heart—a test to navigate the darkness within and the painful truth that awaited her acknowledgment.

For in the shadows of her fractured mind, Jim held the key to her healing—a journey that demanded she face her fears and uncover the strength that lay buried beneath the weight of silence.

CHAPTER 17:
MORNING AFTER

Soft morning light crept through the grimy window of the bed and breakfast, illuminating the sparsely furnished room with its peeling wallpaper and tacky decor. The atmosphere hung thick with tension, laden with unspoken words that neither occupant seemed ready to voice.

Peter lay on one side of the double bed, tension evident in the rigid line of his body. Lucy sat on the opposite edge, staring blankly at the wall as if it might offer answers to questions she hadn't yet formulated. Silence blanketed the room, each heavy heartbeat echoing the emotional distance between them.

A melancholic melody played softly from the clock radio on the nightstand, the sweetness of the melody creating a stark contrast with the reality of their situation. The irony wasn't lost on either of them.

The camera of Lucy's mind pulled back, allowing her to observe their contrasting expressions as if from a distance—Peter's furrowed brow suggesting frustration and conflicted emotions, while her own hollow gaze reflected an emptiness, a sense of loss she couldn't quite articulate.

Lucy fidgeted with a loose thread on the faded bedspread, the void of silence worsening with each passing moment. She opened her mouth, hesitated, and then closed it again. Her inner turmoil battled against the unexpected grip of the antipsychotics she had taken the night before—there were no voices now, just an aching stillness that felt almost as unsettling as the cacophony she had grown accustomed to.

Her eyes darted to Peter, hoping for a hint of connection, an opening to bridge the chasm that had formed between them. But he remained distant, lost in his own thoughts, bracing against the unease that had settled over them like a heavy blanket.

'I need to say something...' she thought, the words barely a whisper in her mind. 'But what if it only makes things worse?'

Peter shifted uncomfortably beside her, the weight of the moment pressing down on him. He glanced at Lucy, catching her eye briefly before looking away. The avoidance felt like a wall growing thicker between them with each moment of silence.

"Just breathe... just keep it together," he muttered to himself, the words barely audible over the music that continued to play, its gentle melody a cruel reminder of the connection they had briefly shared before everything had fallen apart.

He raised his hands, rubbing the nape of his neck as he struggled to muster the courage to speak. But the words failed him, swallowed by the awkwardness that filled the air. The song echoed softly around them, amplifying the longing for connection that sat between them like an unbridgeable canyon.

Finally, Peter rose from the bed, avoiding Lucy's gaze as he grabbed his jacket and headed for the door. He stepped into the dingy lobby, an overwhelming sense of loneliness clinging to him like a wet coat on a winter day.

The receptionist, a woman in her forties with an expression of practiced indifference, barely glanced up from her magazine as he walked past, her disinterest echoing the lack of care evident in the peeling wallpaper and stained carpet. Peter pushed through the front door, stepping out into the grey light outside. It felt like an escape—just enough distance from the tense silence to allow him to breathe again.

He walked aimlessly for a few minutes before spotting a tiny corner shop run by an elderly Indian man in his seventies, his crooked smile a small beacon of warmth in the otherwise dreary street. The bell jingled as Peter entered, but there was a sense of emptiness that lingered inside, matching his own hollow feeling. He meandered down the aisles, scanning the shelves without really seeing their contents.

His eyes caught sight of a few old Nokia phones—smaller, simpler models that would be easier to hide from the prying eyes of modern technology. They represented a simpler time, before smartphones could track your every movement, before digital footprints became nearly impossible to erase. He laughed to himself, then berated himself for being stupid. A burner phone? How much lower could he stoop? Is that who he had become? A man hiding in the shadows, and for what?

'What if it all turns to ash?' Peter wondered as he examined one of the phones. 'Would she still want me if she saw this side of me? And why do I care?'

He purchased two Nokia 3310s, paying in cash to avoid any traceable trails. The old shopkeeper nodded knowingly as he handed over the boxes, as though he had seen too many lives unravel in his years behind the counter to be surprised by a cash transaction for outdated technology.

Peter's journey continued as he drove to a small hardware store, pulling into the parking lot with a sense of purpose that had been lacking earlier. Inside, he felt a strange clarity wash over him. He pulled out his iPhone, carefully disabling all tracking options—becoming a digital ghost while still maintaining a thread of connection to the world.

He searched for "how to disable the safety on a nail gun," watching as quick, easy answers unfurled before him on the screen. Each search term pulled him deeper into a moral grey area, yet he couldn't stop himself from continuing down this path.

After reading through the results, he collected himself and headed for the nail gun section, anxiety flaring in his chest with each step. He grabbed the cheapest nail gun available, a box of nails, and paid cash—no questions asked, no paper trail left behind.

As he exited the store, the weight of his decisions settled heavily on his shoulders. His thoughts spiralled between protection and the tightening grip of desperation that had led him to this point.

"What am I doing?" He asked himself bitterly. 'Am I really capable of this?'

The question hung unanswered as he returned to his car, placing his purchases on the passenger seat before starting the engine. As Peter drove back to the B&B, his hands trembled on the steering wheel. "What the hell am I doing?" he muttered to himself. "Buying burner phones and a nail gun? I'm turning into some kind of criminal. And for what? For a girl I barely know, who's probably going to get us both killed." He glanced at the nail gun in the passenger seat, a wave of nausea washing over him. 'This is insane,' he thought. 'I should just turn around, drive away, and forget I ever met her. Save myself while I still can.' But then he thought of Lucy's face—her vulnerability, her fear, her desperate need for someone to believe in her. "No," he said aloud, "I can't do that. I made a promise. And besides...

what else do I have to live for?" A dark smile crossed his lips. "Maybe this is exactly what I need. A chance to feel alive again, even if it's just for a little while."

Meanwhile, back at the bed and breakfast, Lucy sat on the edge of the bed, coiled tight with anxiety. Each tick of the bedside clock felt deafening in the echoing silence, and it had been hours since Peter had left—a chasm of missed communication stretching wider with each passing minute.

She glanced at the empty space beside her, uncertainty gnawing at her insides. Her thoughts swirled in the unusual quiet of her mind, the lack of Jim's voice and other hallucinations leaving a vacuum that felt almost as disorienting as their presence.

'Did I mess it all up?' She wondered, anxiety tightening her chest. 'Is he ever coming back?'

The questions plagued her as she waited, the minutes stretching into hours until finally, as night began to fall, and she heard footsteps in the hallway outside.

Peter walked back into the room, the eerie stillness wrapping around him like a cloak as he entered. He carried his purchases—the nail gun and phones—his face a mask of determination tinged with emptiness.

He let the bags slip from his hands, the items clattering to the floor in a sound that seemed thunderous in the quiet room. Lucy looked up, her eyes wide with anticipation and fear. Peter stared at her with a look in his eyes that Lucy had never seen before. Was it fear? Was it disgust? It was probably both, Lucy thought.

"When you're ready..." Peter said, exhaling deeply, "we need to talk about last night."

A heavy silence ensued, thick with unspoken words. Lucy's heart raced, uncertainty flooding her features as their future together hung delicately in the balance. The air was charged with tension as Peter stood in the doorway, his gaze locked on Lucy, waiting for her response.

"I'm sorry..." Lucy finally said, her voice trembling with emotion. "For hitting you. It won't happen again." She paused, swallowing hard. "Thank you for picking up the medication."

Her eyes searched his, sincerity etched across her features. She felt vulnerable, laying bare the remnants of her turmoil and hoping he would understand.

"Its fine," Peter replied, nodding as he accepted her apology. "I get it. But I've put an old friend in danger trying to protect you."

The confession hung heavy between them. He ran a hand through his dishevelled hair, beginning to unravel in genuine concern as he continued.

"I was... alarmed when Graham gave me his entire month's supply of pills," he admitted. "I just took them, you know? I didn't want to argue."

A moment of silence enveloped them, the air stifled with unspoken fears. Yet a tentative warmth began to creep back in as they navigated through the aftermath of their conflict, each searching for a way forward.

Lucy breached the gap between them, standing and moving toward Peter until their foreheads were almost touching. In an instinctive gesture, he wrapped his arms around her, pulling her close. A quick kiss passed between them, a silent agreement that despite everything, they wanted to work through this together.

The embrace felt like coming home after being lost in a storm—imperfect, complicated, but somehow right in its imperfection. Whatever lay ahead, for now, they had found their way back to each other in the silence of a dingy bed and breakfast room, their future uncertain but faced together. As they embraced, Peter's eyes darted around the room to confirm that the door was locked. Even though he loved Lucy, he didn't trust her... no, he didn't trust the voices in her head.

The embrace felt like coming home after being lost in a storm—imperfect, complicated, but somehow right in its imperfection. Whatever lay ahead, for now, they had found their way back to each other in the silence of a dingy bed and breakfast room, their future uncertain but faced together.

Chapter 18:
Ghosts from the Past

Later that evening, Peter exited the B&B room, a flicker of determination igniting in his eyes as he stepped into the cool night air. He pulled out one of the burner phones he'd purchased earlier, the weight of recent events drawing him back to old habits he'd hoped to leave behind. He hesitated briefly before dialling Frederick, his old friend, hoping to find solace in a familiar voice from his past.

But there was no answer. The silence on the line gnawed at him, leaving him feeling desperate and impatient as he waited for a connection that didn't come.

Then, just as he began to lose hope, his smartphone buzzed in his pocket. A message from Graham appeared on the screen: "Have you heard about Frederick? Search his name online."

Peter's heart raced, curiosity piquing despite his better judgment. He quickly switched the SIM card from the burner to his smartphone and opened an anonymous browser, fingers trembling slightly as he typed in Frederick's name.

A video thumbnail glowed ominously on the screen, the title alone sending dread rippling through Peter's body. He clicked it open, and his perspective shifted wildly as the reality of what he was seeing sank in.

On-screen, Frederick stood frozen in place, confronted by a determined woman in what was clearly a sting operation. The situation spiralled into an uncomfortable revelation as charges against him were laid bare—explicit images and illicit conversations with young girls. Each word slammed into Peter like a cold wave of realization about who his friend truly was.

Frederick's body language betrayed a mixture of humiliation, paranoia, and depression as he was confronted with evidence of his crimes. Peter's stomach churned as he processed his old friend's actions. A deep-seated disgust filled him, layered with a strange, uncomfortable empathy for Frederick's bleak situation—not for what he had done, but for the person Peter had once believed him to be.

The video progressed, showing no attempts by Frederick to flee the scene. It crescendoed to a brutal climax—Frederick being dragged down, manhandled by a policeman, his colleagues witnessing the spectacle in horrified silence.

Peter's insides twisted, caught between anger and sorrow, frustration at not being able to numb his pain with his usual vices, and an overwhelming urge to sever all ties with this part of his past. He shut off the video, unable to watch anymore, his mind reeling with the implications.

When Peter returned to the B&B room, he felt disoriented, as if the ground beneath him had shifted. Lucy sensed immediately that something was off as he dropped onto the couch beside her. The weight of unprocessed emotions loomed large between them, taking form in a heavy silence neither seemed able to break.

In desperate need of relief from the turmoil in his mind, Peter reached into his pocket, his fingers grazing the car keys—a portal to temporary escape. Without much explanation to Lucy, he drove to the nearest off-license, emerging minutes later with crates of cheap lager. The alcohol represented a catalyst—a way to escape the reality that hounded them both.

The atmosphere in the B&B room transformed into a haze of laughter and cheers as both Peter and Lucy indulged in the drinks, a kaleidoscope of colours swirling around them as the alcohol took effect, making everything blurry and dizzying. The bitter lager loosened the tension between them, their inhibitions falling away like autumn leaves in a strong wind.

They fell into each other in a heated embrace, their passions spilling over into drunken sex—raw, frantic, and unrestrained. For a few hours, they escaped the reality of their situation, finding solace in physical connection when words failed them.

Morning arrived with harsh sunlight filtering through the thin curtains, a cruel reminder of their reckless night. The room resembled a battlefield of discarded beer cans, with fresh vomit staining the carpet in sporadic patches, the stench of stale alcohol lingering in the stagnant air. Both Peter and Lucy were slumped together on the bed, hair a dishevelled mess, faces pale with the aftermath of excessive drinking.

Lucy suddenly bolted upright, groaning as she snatched a small wastebasket from beside the bed, retching violently into it. Peter lurched toward the bathroom, his body rebelling against the previous night's excesses, vomiting painfully into the toilet.

In their shared agony, self-pity reigned supreme. Amidst the chaos of their hangover, a sliver of realization dawned on Peter. Grabbing the nail gun—heavy and ominous in his hands—he fumbled with the nails, his pounding headache complicating each attempt. Finally achieving success, he removed the safety mechanism and placed the weapon within easy reach beneath the bed.

"At some point, they'll come for us," he muttered under his breath, the paranoia of their situation never entirely absent from his mind. But the thought was quickly followed by urgency as he rushed back to the toilet to heave again, his body still purging the previous night's excesses.

They eventually slipped into a deep sleep, the world around them fading to a blur as their bodies demanded rest. When the next morning approached, they woke slightly more coherent, the basics of survival nudging them toward the gross-looking restaurant area downstairs. They stumbled down to face a greasy, unappealing fry-up breakfast, but hunger dictated their needs despite the questionable appearance of the food.

The stench of vomit still clung to them as they ascended back to their room afterward, the faces of despair following closely behind. They settled on the bed, the tension returning as Peter grabbed the remote, flicking on the small TV that sat on the dresser opposite.

The screen flickered with social commentary, an upbeat narrative painting a picture of hope and progress that stood in stark contrast to the heaviness closing in around them.

"Why the fuck are you here?" Lucy asked suddenly, her voice cutting through the drone of the television in an unexpected moment of clarity.

Peter turned to her, confusion evident on his face. "What do you mean?"

Lucy's expression scrunched with frustration, something clearly bubbling to the surface that she had been holding back.

"It's not even about the punch!" she exclaimed, her voice rising. "Why are you here, Peter? I'm ruining your life. You're on the run, and this isn't going to end well."

His heart sank at her words; he couldn't explain the connection sparking between them, the pull of something deeper that kept him by her side despite the circumstances.

"I… I don't know," he admitted, his voice small. "I think I like you."

Lucy snapped, her voice rising in intensity. "For fuck's sake! You're good-looking, a bit awkward, but a nice guy. You'll meet someone else, have a normal fucking life." She paused, her eyes filling with tears. "I can't repay you for what you've done; I need you to leave. Please, don't waste any more of your life in this cesspit. It's been so intense, and I feel like I love you... but I really want you to go."

Her words hung in the air, enveloping them in a mixture of desperation and longing. The distance between them felt insurmountable, yet there was an undeniable thread weaving through this fractured connection—something neither of them fully understood but both felt acutely.

The gentle rays of morning sunlight continued to filter through the tattered curtains, casting a soft, almost haunting glow across the cluttered room. They lay entwined in bed, the remnants of their chaotic night still echoing in the hushed silence. Lucy's face was buried in the crook of Peter's neck, her eyes closed as she took solace in the warmth of his presence. Tears had dried on her cheeks, remnants of yesterday's emotional turmoil.

Peter stared at the ceiling, his thoughts racing as the weight of Lucy's desperate words hung uncomfortably between them. A mixture of guilt and cowardice weighed heavily on his heart, preventing him from addressing what they both knew to be true.

"Do you think we can ever go back?" Lucy asked softly, breaking the silence that had settled between them.

Peter glanced at her, his heart racing. He opened his mouth to respond, but the words dissolved into uncertainty, the same cowardice prevailing. Instead, he pulled her closer, desperately seeking comfort in the physical connection as a temporary escape from reality. But guilt festered at the back of his mind, impossible to entirely ignore. He couldn't admit to her—or even to himself—that he was terrified of being alone again. That the thought of returning to his empty apartment, his meaningless job, and his hollow existence was more frightening than whatever danger lay ahead. He needed her, not because he was a good person or wanted to save her, but because she was the only thing standing between him and the abyss.

'Just a little while longer...' he thought, trying to reassure himself. 'We're safe here for now.'

As silence blanketed them once more, Peter's resolve weakened. He sat up abruptly, running a hand through his hair, frustration etching lines across his brow. The cozy atmosphere shifted, becoming heavy with tension. Lucy's eyes fluttered open, confusion shadowing her face at his sudden movement.

Reality could no longer be ignored. Peter rummaged through his wallet and Lucy's purse, the urgency of their situation finally dawning on him. He pulled out crumpled bills, counting rapidly—the total barely reaching £150.

"Three days," he murmured to himself, the reality of their situation hitting him with full force. "Three days at most."

He shook his head, wrestling with the hopelessness, the reality of being trapped in a cycle of self-destruction closing in fast. He glanced at Lucy, who had sat up in bed, concern crossing her features.

"What's wrong?" she asked, pulling the sheet around herself.

His anxiety blossomed as the reflection of their poverty set in. Desperation gnawed at him—a confrontation with their reality was inevitable and could no longer be postponed.

"We can't stay here like this," he said, his voice tight with stress. "Something has to change."

Before Lucy could respond, there was a sudden, loud bang at the door—a visceral shock cutting through the morning quiet. The sound echoed through the small room, freezing them both in place.

Chapter 19:
Point of No Return

Two police officers in their early thirties, dressed in full SWAT uniform, barrelled in without knocking, storming past the threshold with intent, guns drawn. The atmosphere instantly shifted from mundane tension to electrifying danger.

"Lucy Evans! Hands where we can see them!" the first officer commanded, his voice authoritative and sharp.

Lucy's eyes widened in sudden panic. She instinctively raised her hands above her head, fear coursing through her veins like ice water. Peter dropped the wallet he'd been holding, instinct kicking in, his hands trembling visibly. He lowered his head, trying to hide from the storm of chaos crashing in around them.

"It's not what you think!" Lucy cried, her voice trembling with fear.

The officers advanced, weapons positioned, tension thick in the air. The sterile click of firearms being readied ignited a primal fight-or-flight response in both of them.

"Lucy, just stay calm," Peter whispered, his voice resolute despite the fear evident in his eyes.

As the officers moved towards them, an intense focus formed in Peter's expression. The sheer desperation of the moment gave way to something darker as his hand reached beneath the bed, fingers closing around the handle of the nail gun he'd hidden there.

In an unexpected burst of adrenaline, Peter lunged forward, a dark shape moving too fast for Lucy to fully process. She heard a series of loud cracks, like rapid-fire explosions, and a scream that was swiftly cut short. The scene became a blur of motion, the air thick with a metallic scent that made her stomach churn. Had he fired the nail gun? Was that even real?

A high-pitched ringing filled her ears, drowning out all other sounds as the world tilted violently. She saw flashes of colour—red, black, blue—intermingling in a dizzying kaleidoscope. The officers were moving, shifting, their faces contorted into grotesque masks of anger and pain. Or were they?

"Peter! NO!" she screamed, but her voice seemed distant, muffled as if she were underwater.

The reality of what was happening shattered around them, echoing with chaos and the acrid smell of gunpowder. Lucy threw herself against the wall, unable to process the horror unfolding before her. Peter's vulnerabilities seemed to evaporate, replaced by sheer survival instinct—as fear transmuted to violent urgency in the face of immediate threat.

But amidst the gunfire chaos, Lucy gasped sharply as white-hot pain exploded through her leg. A stray bullet had pierced her thigh, sending agony surging through her body as she screamed.

"It... hurts!" she cried out, clutching at the wound as blood seeped between her fingers.

Peter, too, felt a searing pain in his shoulder as he dove for cover, fists balled in primal compulsion. The reality of their actions dawned on them—the past had never prepared them for this moment; everything now hung on a precipice between life, death, and consequences that would forever alter their existence.

The officers lay sprawled on the floor, blood pooling beneath them, as Lucy and Peter scrambled toward the bodies, urgency pumping adrenaline through their veins, temporarily overriding the pain of their wounds.

Peter snatched the guns from the fallen officers, his movements driven by instinct rather than conscious thought. Through ragged breaths, Lucy reached for Peter's hand, fear entwining their minds and bodies.

"We need to get the keys... the van outside!" Lucy insisted, her voice determined despite the chaos surrounding them.

They urgently dragged the bodies aside, their hearts racing, sensing more police would soon arrive. The weight of desperation drove them to action, fingers fumbling over money and weapons found in the officers' pockets, gathering what they could use for their escape.

There was no turning back now. In the span of mere minutes, they had crossed a line that could never be uncrossed, their fates sealed by actions born of desperation and fear. All that remained was the instinct to survive, to run, and to find some way forward in a world that had suddenly become infinitely more dangerous for them both.

Chapter 20:
The Escape

They stormed through the B&B lobby, adrenaline propelling them forward despite their injuries. The receptionist—the same forty-something woman with the perpetually bored expression—glanced up from her magazine, her eyes widening in shock at their dishevelled appearance and the blood staining their clothes.

"What on Earth...?" she began, rising halfway from her seat.

Peter attempted to suppress her reaction, frantically fumbling for a solution. He thrust a wad of cash at her, urgency making his voice rough and commanding.

"Keep this quiet!" he said breathlessly. "We need a ride to the train station... now!"

The receptionist's initial shock gave way to understanding as her eyes fell on the cash—enough money to make looking the other way worth her while. She nodded hesitantly, recognizing the fear in their eyes and choosing, for whatever reason, not to ask questions.

"I'll... I'll see what I can do," she muttered, reaching for her phone.

Fifteen minutes later, they arrived at the train station, huddled together with breaths heavy from adrenaline and pain. Lucy's leg throbbed where the bullet had grazed her, and Peter's shoulder burned, but neither dared seek medical attention. The atmosphere around them buzzed with commuters going about their normal day, oblivious to the chaos that had engulfed the two fugitives.

They rushed to a nearby shop, hastily purchasing supplies—a cheap razor, shaving cream, and hair dye. With these minimal disguise materials in hand, they stumbled into the public restroom, urgency and fear clashing in every movement.

The fluorescent lights buzzed above them, flickering as they dove into the process of transforming their appearances. Lucy shaved one side of her head completely, then dyed the remaining hair beach blonde. Each stroke of the razor and brush echoed a desperate wish for anonymity, for escape from the consequences racing toward them.

Peter, eyes glued to the mirror, shaved his head completely bald and removed all of his beard except for a distinctive moustache, which he also dyed beach blonde. Each snip of the scissors and buzz of the razor felt like shedding their former selves, leaving behind the chaos of their past identities.

Their reflections showed how they had morphed into shadows that might blend with the crowd—relics of their former lives now hidden within the noise and flow of anonymous travellers.

Across the tracks, a train pulled in, the destination sign flickering invitingly. They exchanged a glance, their eyes filled with the stark realization that there was no turning back from what they had done.

"This is it..." Lucy whispered, her voice a breathless mixture of worry and desperate hope.

Peter gripped her hand tightly, pulling her close to his side. "Let's go," he said resolutely.

As they were about to step onto the train, the world around Lucy suddenly shifted. Jim's voice cut through her consciousness with jarring clarity.

'You sure you want to do that, sweetheart?' He whispered in her mind.

The scene before her morphed and dissolved. The train station disappeared, replaced by an oncoming car, its horn blaring deafeningly as it approached her at alarming speed. Lucy froze, paralyzed by confusion as reality and hallucination blurred together. The car grazed against her hand just as she felt herself yanked forcefully backward by Peter.

The world snapped back into focus. Lucy found herself not at the train station at all, but standing in the middle of the main road outside the B&B car park. The car that had nearly hit her managed to slow down sufficiently to avoid serious injury, but her arm stung where it had made contact.

In the distance, the driver put two fingers up in a crude gesture as he drove away, his anger at her carelessness evident even from afar. Peter was yelling at her, his face contorted with concern and frustration, but his words were completely inaudible to her, drowned out by the ringing in her ears and Jim's mocking voice.

'You stupid cunt,' Jim's voice echoed in her mind. 'When did you last take your Olanzapine? Such a princess, always daydreaming your life away.' I can't believe I nearly died, but Peter can't find a way to understand me. Am I just a burden to him?

As Lucy sank down to sit on the curb after nearly being run over, she was stunned into silence. A tear or two ran down her face as the realization hit her—there had been no police raid, no shootout, and no desperate flight to the train station. It had all been a vivid hallucination, another break from reality caused by her failing to take her medication.

The car engine hummed softly in the background as Lucy remained trembling at the edge of the car park, her breath shallow and uneven. The neon sign from the B&B flickered in the distance, casting a haunting glow on her pale face. She was still reeling from the surreal confrontation with Jim's haunting voice and the realization that she had once again lost her grip on reality.

Peter approached cautiously, worry etched deeply on his face. He gently brushed his fingers against her arm, as if afraid she might shatter at his touch.

"Lucy, are you okay?" he asked softly.

Lucy flinched involuntarily, her mind still racing to separate what was real from what she had imagined. She looked away, struggling to piece together her fragmented perception amid the emotional whirlwind inside her.

"I don't know," she admitted, her voice shaky and uncertain. "Everything... feels blurred." Can I ever trust my own mind again? Will I ever be able to live a normal life?

Little did she realize that her vulnerability in that moment drew Peter closer, an unspoken connection forming amidst the chaos of her fractured mind and their complicated circumstances? Theres something here that defies logic, feelings enveloped by a sense of being needed, a strange excitement in the chaos. She can't go through her life alone. I have to do my best to be there for her.

They treaded quietly through the lobby a few minutes later, a marked contrast to the vibrant, chaotic escape she had imagined earlier. The receptionist, still jaded and disinterested, barely glanced up from her book as they passed. Peter moved to Lucy's side, instinctively shielding her from view as they made their way toward the stairs.

Lucy leaned heavily against the wall as they climbed, her heart pounding with exhaustion and lingering fear. The familiar lull of Jim's mocking laughter played softly in the corners of her mind, persistent despite her efforts to silence it.

'You think they can help you?' Jim whispered. 'Just look at yourself.'

Lucy's face paled further as they reached their floor, the weight of his words suffocating what little resolve she had managed to gather.

When they entered their room, Lucy collapsed onto the bed, her body sinking into the worn mattress as if it might swallow her whole. She buried her face in her hands, the moment spiralling into a whirlwind of panic and doubt that threatened to consume her entirely.

Peter hovered nearby, concern etched on his features as he observed her trembling form. He stepped closer, unsure how to help but unwilling to leave her alone in such a state.

"Lucy, breathe," he said carefully, his voice gentle. "Just take a moment. You're safe here."

His voice cut through the malaise that had settled over her, grounding her momentarily. Lucy looked up, her eyes swimming with tears that threatened to spill over at any second.

The world around her felt veiled in a hazy film, shadows dancing at the edges of her vision while Jim's echoes faded but remained unsettlingly present. She swallowed hard, her gaze falling on the medication bottle on the bedside table. The weight of her decision—to take the pills or continue living in her increasingly dangerous delusions—bore down on her with crushing intensity.

"I need to take my meds," she said, her voice trembling with emotion and fear. "I need help."

She reached for the pill vial with shaking hands, struggling to uncap it. Peter watched closely, instinctively stepping forward when he saw her difficulty.

"Here, let me help you with that," he offered gently.

He took the vial from her unsteady grasp, carefully pouring the prescribed dose into her palm. Lucy stared at the pills, her resolve faltering momentarily as Jim's voice made one last attempt to dissuade her.

But this time, she closed her fingers around the medication, determined to reclaim some control over her fractured reality. With Peter's silent support beside her, she raised her hand to her mouth, taking the first step on a long journey back toward stability and clarity.

CHAPTER 21:
TRANSFORMATIONS

Lucy swallowed the pills dry, her throat feeling constricted with the effort. She closed her eyes tightly, willing the waves of despair to recede from her consciousness. Gradually, the panic began to subside, though Jim's echo lingered just below the surface of her thoughts—reminiscent but fainter than before, like a radio station slowly losing signal.

'You think they can heal you?' Jim's voice hissed faintly. 'Foolish girl...'

Lucy shook her head, fighting against the suffocating turmoil within. She looked up at Peter, who stood resolute beside her, his presence somehow managing to be a calming force despite all they had been through.

'This is still just a facade,' she reminded herself silently. 'I need to keep my wits about me. I've got to stay one step ahead.'

She drew in a shaky breath, her voice steadier now when she spoke, yet tinged with an urgency that couldn't be ignored.

"How... how do we change?" she asked, looking up at Peter. "I need to change everything about myself while I'm still breathing."

Peter swallowed hard, the gravity of her words reflected in his expression. A flicker of fear glimmered in his eyes as he considered the implications of what she was suggesting.

"You really think that's the answer?" he asked tentatively. "We don't know if there's any other suspects, and if they track us, there's an implication of guilt." He paused, his forehead creasing with worry. "Do we not bide our time?"

He knelt beside her, a mixture of sympathy and concern etched into his features as he continued. "Lucy, this isn't just about the tramp, or looks, or changing your hair. It's about who you are… beneath everything."

As he spoke, flashes of Lucy's past flickered through her mind—memories of the quiet little girl always waiting for affection that rarely came, the teenager desperately seeking acceptance from anyone who would offer it, moments of self-harm that left trails of blood and pain across her skin. Images from a life spent trying to escape herself, always falling short of finding peace.

Lucy found her voice again, the vulnerability of the moment allowing her to peel away the layers of pretence she usually hid behind.

"I'm tired of being the girl who lives in shadows and fears," she said, frustration evident in her tone. "Maybe I can become someone else, someone new—someone who does not have to look over her shoulder."

Peter watched her closely, conflicted emotions swirling within him. He understood the fragility of her request yet felt the familiar pull of his complicated feelings for her—the desire to protect her warring with the knowledge that some wounds couldn't be healed by simply running away.

"Lucy... it's not that simple," he said hesitantly. "Running may feel like an escape, but it doesn't erase the past."

Her eyes gleamed with a mixture of anger and sorrow. The voice of Jim scratched at the surface of her mind, taunting and belittling, though the medication was beginning to dull its intensity.

She rose from the bed, pacing the small space with renewed determination, needing to move as her thoughts raced.

"I don't expect you to stay, Peter," she whispered, her voice raw with emotion. "You could leave now and have a good life. Find someone who's better than me. Someone unbroken."

She looked at him, almost pleading, hoping to disarm him with her honesty about the depths of her darkness—a confession and an offering of freedom in one breathe.

As she spoke, Peter's thoughts drifted to his own past—moments of profound loneliness, failed relationships that had culminated in deep-seated insecurities about his self-worth. He remembered the countless times he had tried to reach out to others, only to be met with disappointment or rejection. These moments had shaped him, creating the man who now stood before Lucy, drawn to her brokenness perhaps because it mirrored his own.

His chest tightened as he stared into her eyes, recognizing the sincerity there. He opened his mouth to say he would stay, no matter what. He then realised he didn't know what he would do. Why would he ever leave? It was better to be needed, even if it was within the confines of this hell hole than to be lonely. He was a coward, not a hero.

"Lucy, you ARE broken," he acknowledged, his voice wavering slightly. "But I'm not leaving... not yet. We'll figure this out together."

Her breath caught momentarily as he leaned closer, sharing the weight of his confession. Lucy noticed the sincerity in his eyes—a promise of solidarity, a united front against their shared demons. It wasn't the blind optimism of someone who didn't understand her struggles, but the measured commitment of someone who recognized her damage and chose to stay anyway.

After a moment of silence heavy with unspoken understanding, Peter gathered the supplies from the floor, his head filled with thoughts of what might come next. They shared a meaningful glance before he gestured toward the bathroom sink.

"Alright then," he said, suddenly animated with purpose. "How about we plan this differently? Let's give you a new look… we can work on it together. Make it… a fresh start."

Lucy looked hopeful for the first time in days, her grip on her own fate shifting from despair toward possibility.

The air in the small bathroom was thick with excitement and nervousness as they stood in front of the mirror. Lucy lifted up a pack of hair dye, casting a hopeful glance towards Peter.

"I've always wanted to change my hair," she admitted, her voice uncertain but determined. "If we do this, it might finally feel like I can step into a new version of myself."

Peter nodded, picking up the supplies as they positioned themselves before the mirror.

'Maybe this will be the turning point for both of us,' he thought to himself. 'A chance to carve out a new identity from the wreckage. But will it really change anything?'

As they started dyeing her hair, the chemistry between them crackled with energy. The air was charged—almost electric—as Lucy's hair gradually transformed into a bright hue of vibrant blue. What had begun as a practical measure of disguise evolved into something more significant—a declaration of change, of breaking free from the person she had been.

Echoes of unexpected laughter eventually morphed into comfortable silence as the transformation unfolded, somehow solidifying their bond amid the fear and uncertainty that surrounded them. Each stroke of the brush carried the weight of promises yet unspoken, a symbolic severing from their pasts and the creation of something new.

As Peter finished, he took a step back to admire their handywork, a small smile playing across his lips.

"Beautiful..." he murmured, his eyes fixed not just on her transformed appearance but on Lucy herself.

They locked eyes, the moment heavy with resolve and vulnerability. Lucy took a deep breath, the air swirling with possibility inside the dimly lit bathroom.

"I'm ready to face whatever comes next," she said, her voice trembling but hopeful.

They stood before one another, a sense of unity blooming between them as they shared a moment of quiet intimacy—two broken souls attempting to reconstruct their identities and redefine what it meant to belong together in a world that often felt like it was against them.

As they lingered in that moment of connection, the distant sounds of police sirens could be heard faintly in the background—a stark reminder of the chaos waiting for them outside, a signal that their journey was far from over.

The danger remained, but for now, in this small space they had created for themselves, they had found a moment of peace and purpose that neither had expected.

Lucy's blue hair dripped slightly onto her shoulders, marking her with the physical manifestation of her desire for change. Whatever came next, she would face it as someone new—or at least, someone trying to become new. The medication, the dye, Peter's presence—none of these things could erase her past, but together they offered the possibility of a different future than the one she had been hurtling toward.

Beneath the makeover and shared vulnerability, a question lingered unspoken between them: was transformation truly possible, or were they merely changing their appearance while their essential natures remained unchanged? Only time would reveal the answer, but for now, the act of trying was enough to kindle a spark of hope in both their hearts.

Chapter 22:
The Escape

Lucy and Peter stood by the grimy window of their B&B room, staring out into the night. The sounds of police sirens echoed in the distance while the flashing lights from several patrol cars pulsed against the dull walls, casting eerie blue and red shadows across their faces. They watched, hearts pounding, as the vehicles veered past the building, a shared breath of relief escaping them when it became clear the police weren't stopping.

"Are they... are they even looking for us?" Lucy whispered, her eyes wide with lingering fear despite the medication dulling her paranoia.

Peter, already leaning against the wall, shifted slightly, uncertainty etched on his face. "I don't think so... not yet," he said quietly. "But we can't stick around to find out."

The sirens faded into the distance, leaving a heavy silence in their wake. A moment passed, filled with unspoken tension as they both processed the fleeting sense of safety and the knowledge that it could vanish in an instant.

They moved away from the window and sat at a small, wobbly table, their faces illuminated by the dim overhead light. Several crumpled notes lay scattered before them, their future hanging precariously in the balance along with their dwindling finances.

"We need to come up with a plan," Lucy said with determination, her newly dyed hair framing her face. "We have to get out of here... far away from my home."

Peter nodded, his expression hardening with resolve as he started counting their diminishing amount of money.

"What about that seaside town?" he suggested after a moment. "The one at the top of the country? It's several hours away from here."

Lucy's eyes lit up at the suggestion. "Yeah... it's remote enough that no one would think to look for us there."

They leaned closer together, the energy between them shifting as they began to brainstorm their escape in earnest, their voices low but animated with a newfound purpose.

"If we spend the last of our money on a cab," Peter continued, "we can get to that town... then find a crappy pub or inn."

"And work behind the bar to cover our lodging," Lucy added, the plan taking shape in her mind. "That way, we can get food, drink, and a roof over our heads without arousing suspicion." Lucy quickly reassembled her old smart phone to search for a B&B no one would ever think to look for them at the other side of the country, although she thought she had masked her Ip location, there was a triangle with an eye at its centre over the search engine. The results to her search were being manipulated but for what, and by who?

Lucy bit her lip, her determination growing as Peter's plan took on more concrete details. The medication was helping her think more clearly than she had in days, the voices in her head reduced to distant murmurs rather than the deafening chorus they had been.

A short while later, Peter approached the reception desk with a mixture of anxiety and determination. The receptionist—the same woman in her forties, weary but curious—looked up from her magazine, sensing something was amiss but saying nothing.

"Can you help us book a cab to the seaside town tonight?" Peter asked firmly. "It's urgent."

The receptionist raised an eyebrow but nodded, reaching for the phone, her actions brisk and businesslike. Lucy watched from a distance, her heart racing, as Peter settled their remaining tab with some of the precious cash they had left.

With the cab booked and the arrangements made, Lucy and Peter stood at the entrance of the B&B, their meagre belongings stuffed into bags slung over their shoulders. Despite the uncertainty shrouding them, a renewed sense of purpose infused their movements.

"This is it, then," Lucy said, taking a deep breath. "A fresh start."

They exchanged a look that contained a mixture of anxiety and a strange spark of hope flickering between them, a connection neither had expected to find in the midst of such chaos.

As the cab pulled up, its headlights casting long shadows over the pavement, both Lucy and Peter hesitated for a brief moment, looking back at the B&B—the reluctant prison that had nonetheless provided them sanctuary when they needed it most.

"No looking back," Peter said softly. "Just forward from here on out."

With that simple declaration, they climbed into the backseat. The cab driver glanced at them briefly through the rearview mirror—an indifferent stranger who asked no questions—while Lucy and Peter settled in, grappling with the gravity of their leap into the unknown.

On the side of the cab read Sapphire taxi services, though this had gone unnoticed by the couple, had they paid attention to detail they may have been more savvy to future events. The cab pulled away from the curb, leaving the dim B&B behind. Lucy glanced at Peter, a soft smile breaking through her anxiety—a glimmer of hope among the chaos they were fleeing.

"Whatever happens from here on out... we're in it together, right?" she asked tentatively, seeking reassurance.

Peter gave her an earnest nod, their eyes locking as the cab barrelled down the quiet roads, dim buildings fading into the night behind them. The unspoken promise between them offered a comfort neither had expected to find when their paths had first crossed.

The cab rolled into the seaside town several hours later, its headlights illuminating the deserted streets. The atmosphere was heavy, an eerie silence blanketing everything around them. Buildings loomed on either side, uninviting and drab, resembling a great council estate that time had forgotten. Paint flaked from weathered walls, a testament to years of neglect and the harsh coastal elements.

Lucy and Peter stepped out of the cab, glancing around at their new surroundings. Their expressions revealed a mixture of anxiety and uncertainty as the wind bit at their faces, carrying the sharp scent of salt and decay. The air felt thick, charged with foreboding, as if the town itself were warning them away.

They wandered the empty streets for a while, searching for somewhere—anywhere—that might offer them work and shelter. Eventually, they stumbled across a run-down pub called "The Trout Inn," mockingly illuminated by flickering fluorescent lights. The sign creaked ominously as it swung slightly in the wind, half the paint peeled away, revealing faded letters beneath. It looked like a dive—one of the roughest establishments either of them had ever seen.

An ominous melody about finality and doom played softly from somewhere inside as they approached the entrance, the music underlining their trepidation alongside a strange, twisted excitement. Lucy looked up at Peter, the hesitance in their shared gaze palpable. They exchanged a silent understanding, the tension thick in the air between them. A sense of danger lingered around the building, and doubt crept into their minds, yet the need for shelter and work drove them forward regardless.

They pushed the door open, its hinges screaming a rusty protest. Inside, The Trout Inn reeked of stale beer and desperation, its decay a tapestry of water stains and cigarette burns. Lucy and Peter's expressions hardened as they scanned the room, each detail a warning etched in grime. In the far corner, a drunken old man sat nursing a beer, seemingly oblivious to their presence. The scene was undoubtedly foreboding, a stark reminder that outsiders might not be welcomed in this forgotten corner of the country.

Despite their instincts screaming at them to turn back, they approached the bar with determined steps. The atmosphere hung heavy around them, anticipation palpable in the stale air. Crickets chirped through the open windows while the low hum of the flickering lights provided an unsettling soundtrack to their arrival.

They stood at the bar, waiting for service. After a moment, a manager appeared—a rugged man in his mid-fifties with several missing teeth, his presence imposing as he emerged from a back room. He sized them up with a look that suggested he had seen his fair share of trouble and perhaps caused some of it himself.

"What'll it be then?" he asked gruffly, his voice matching the rough appearance of the establishment.

Peter swallowed hard, fighting against the oppressive atmosphere as he placed their order. "Two Fosters, please," he said, his voice nervous but steady. After a brief pause, he added, "And, uh... do you have any accommodation available? We're looking for work."

The manager raised an eyebrow, an amused grin forming on his weathered face as he considered the request.

"Work, huh?" he replied, looking them over once more. "You're lucky; there's a shift tonight you both can cover. After accommodations are deducted, you'll be earning about ten quid each a night. Food and drinks included, but don't take liberties."

Peter exchanged a quick glance with Lucy, the tension in the air heavy but softening slightly with the promise of a potential lifeline. The manager motioned toward a dim corridor, his expression revealing a hint of caution or perhaps warning as he led them away from the main bar area.

As they followed him down the poorly lit hallway, anxiety settled deeper in their chests. They arrived at a door marked "ROOM 2," and the manager swung it open without ceremony. He stepped aside, revealing a space even grimier than their previous accommodations—a small, worn-down room that seemed to hold stories best left untold.

Inside, a small mattress lay directly on the floor, stained and thin. The dim light flickered overhead, casting unnerving shadows across ripped, dirty carpeting. The decay was overwhelming, with graffiti lacing the walls and a pungent odour lingering in the air—a mixture of mould, cigarette smoke, and other less identifiable scents.

The manager pointed to the corner, where a makeshift toilet sat—an unsettling sight that made Lucy's stomach churn. There was no toilet seat, and the surrounding walls were decorated with crude symbols and messages, remnants of a violent past that seemed to whisper warnings through the peeling paint.

As they settled into their squalid room at The Trout Inn, Peter couldn't shake the feeling that they had made a terrible mistake. "This place is a shithole," he muttered, staring at the stained mattress on the floor. "We should have kept driving. Tried to find somewhere better."

But he knew that wasn't true. They were out of money, out of options. This was all they had left. He looked at Lucy, her face pale and drawn in the dim light, a wave of tenderness washing over him. "It'll be alright," he said, forcing a smile. "We'll make it work. We always do."

But inside, he wondered if they were simply delaying the inevitable. Sooner or later, they would be caught, either by the police or by their own demons. And when that happened, he knew he would be the one to pay the price. "But maybe," he thought, "maybe it'll be worth it, if it means keeping her safe, for just a little while longer."

Lucy gripped Peter's arm instinctively, fear evident in her wide eyes. "Is this really where we're staying?" she asked breathlessly, unable to hide her dismay.

Yet, beneath the dread and disgust that the room inspired, a strange flicker of hope ignited between them. They were in this together—this felt like a fresh start, twisted and marred as it was, but perhaps it held some promise of a future away from the dangers they had fled.

"It's not ideal," Peter whispered resolutely, "but it's a start. Together, we can make it work."

They shared a moment of connection, the weight of their choices hanging in the air around them, yet a spark of determination glimmered between them. In the shadows of despair, they clung to one another, ready to forge a new path in their hidden sanctuary—their fragile alliance amplifying the flicker of resilience amidst the decay surrounding them.

The following day found them behind the bar of The Trout Inn, the worn wooden surface scarred from years of use and abuse. The pub remained dimly lit even in daylight, its ambiance heavy and oppressive. Lucy and Peter shared a nervous glance as they familiarized themselves with their new workplace, both feeling the weight of their decision to remain in this dismal establishment.

The manager strode behind the bar, the cynicism etched into his face seemingly permanent. He grinned at the two newcomers, his eyes glinting with a hint of mischief as he prepared to brief them on their duties.

"Alright, listen up," he said with a raspy chuckle. "Tonight's 'Pound in the Pot,' so you'd better brace yourselves. Stripper comes in at nine, and the locals love to put a pound in for a peep."

Lucy's eyes widened in surprise at this information. Before they could fully process the implications of what the night would bring, the door to the pub swung open, admitting a stunning woman probably in her late twenties, maybe early thirties, with the kind of Eastern European beauty that catches your eye even when it's a bit worn. Her blonde hair was dyed, darker roots just visible, and her makeup was heavy, trying a bit too hard to cover the shadows under her eyes. You could see faint track marks on her arms through the thin fabric of her cheap, sparkly dress—a testament to the desperation that likely drove her to take this gig. She sauntered across the grimy floor, her expression a mix of weariness and practiced confidence, like she'd done this a hundred times before and knew exactly what to expect.

The stark contrast between the newcomer's pristine appearance and the dreary decor of The Trout Inn only emphasized the surreal nature of the situation Lucy and Peter had found themselves in. As they exchanged uncertain glances, both wondered what other surprises this strange new chapter in their lives might hold—and whether they had jumped from one dangerous situation into another equally precarious one.

Chapter 23:
The Trout Inn

The manager smirked at Lucy's obvious discomfort, clearly pleased with the effect of both his announcement and the blonde woman's entrance. He addressed them with a glint of something unsettling in his eyes.

"Don't fuck anything up, alright?" he said, grinning widely. "I'm off for the night."

He strode away without waiting for a response, leaving Peter and Lucy to manage the bar on their own. Lucy swallowed hard, anxiety creeping in as the atmosphere thickened around them. They were completely on their own now, in unfamiliar territory with no safety net.

Night fell quickly, the streets outside growing eerily quiet as darkness descended. The bar remained a sanctuary for a handful of locals who seemed to materialize as the evening progressed. Three men sat at the bar, their presence heavy and somewhat threatening. One of them, Larry—a wiry, twitchy man in his mid-thirties—showed clear signs of hyperactivity, his fingers constantly drumming on the bar surface as his eyes darted around the room.

The old man Lucy had noticed when they first arrived leaned against the far end of the bar, unashamedly eyeing the stripper who was perched on the bar top, completely naked except for a pair of high heels. She wore a sly grin as the old man inched closer, but suddenly shoved him away with surprising force, holding her ground without showing any real aggression.

"Not interested, mate," she said firmly but with a playful edge to her voice that suggested she'd had plenty of practice rejecting unwanted advances.

Lucy's fingers tightened around the damp bar towel; her knuckles white. She watched the exchange, her eyes darting between the men, searching for an escape route she wasn't sure existed. Peter, meanwhile, focused on pouring pints, grateful to have something concrete to occupy his hands and attention.

As the night wore on, Larry turned to Peter, a wide grin plastered across his face, his enthusiasm bordering on manic.

"Oi, mate!" he called out, voice too loud for the small space. "What do you reckon of the view? Lovely girl you got there..."

Peter, still feeling awkward in somewhat intimidating surroundings, forcing a smile as he responded. "It's, uh... certainly different," he managed, trying to remain polite while avoiding engagement.

Larry chuckled, leaning on the counter as an unwelcome sense of camaraderie began to build between them. The old man smirked knowingly from his spot at the end of the bar, watching the banter unfold with evident amusement.

"Enjoy it while it lasts, lads," the old man said, leering at them both. "This is a place you won't forget, I promise!"

As Lucy served drinks at the other end of the bar, she discreetly observed Larry, noting the wildness in his eyes that suggested he was under the influence of something stronger than the beer in his glass. Her suspicions were confirmed when Larry disappeared into the restroom, the sounds of his overactive energy echoing down the hallway.

Inside the grimy toilet, Larry pulled out a line of cocaine, preparing to indulge. With practiced movements, he placed a degraded half-coin on the doorframe above the toilet cubicle, a signal to others in the know.

"Welcome to the area, drink up, kids," he murmured to himself with a grin as he snorted a line before rejoining the others, visibly invigorated by the drug.

When Larry emerged, he was beaming with renewed energy. He called out to Peter across the bar, his voice carrying easily in the small space. "Left you a little something in the loo, mate!" he announced loudly.

Peter winced at his volume, aware that the entire bar could hear as Larry's words floated into the air, drawing attention from the other patrons. One man in particular—John, a rough-looking individual in his mid-forties—clearly overheard, his brow furrowing as he leaned back against the wall, assessing the situation.

"What've you got for me then, clown?" John asked sceptically, sizing Larry up with an unfriendly glare.

Larry smiled and sauntered into the restroom again, oblivious to the potential danger or perhaps welcoming it, a glimmer of mischief in his expression. After a moment, he returned to the bar, attempting to maintain a casual demeanour though his excitement was palpable.

The tension in the room grew as John, feeling emboldened, strode toward the restroom, pulling open the door with an air of entitlement. "Just curious," he called back, his tone challenging though he feigned indifference. "What'd you leave for me?"

He disappeared into the stall, and though no one could see him, it was clear what was happening. John took the half-coin down from above the doorframe and snorted the cocaine Larry had left there. When he emerged moments later, a satisfied smile had crept onto his face. He didn't look back at Larry or acknowledge what had just transpired, instead nonchalantly approaching the bar where Peter stood.

"Two pints of Carling, mate," John ordered, his voice steady despite the drug he'd just consumed.

Peter prepared the order, feeling the atmosphere growing thick with tension around him. John took a seat at the bar, scanning the room with keen eyes that missed nothing. His posture exuded a sense of entitlement and control, and the air crackled with unease as he settled in.

As Peter served the pints, he exchanged tight-lipped pleasantries with John, trying to maintain a professional demeanour. The uneasy tension escalated as John's eyes, marked with an unsettling pleasure, flickered over to the stripper who continued to perform for the sparse crowd.

"This is nice..." John remarked casually, taking a long sip of his beer, "but I don't want my money out of this country."

Peter froze momentarily, the weight of John's words settling in his gut like a stone. The statement was clearly meant to provoke, laden with xenophobic implications that made Peter's skin crawl. The air around them grew heavy, charged with potential conflict.

Peter opened his mouth to respond, but words evaded him, swallowed by the fear of confrontation in this unfamiliar territory. Silence hung thick between them, charged with unspoken words and brewing hostility. John's demeanour shifted as he noted Peter's hesitation, his eyes narrowing with predatory interest.

"You think I'm out of order, don't you?" John asked, leaning in closer, his voice low and confrontational.

Maintained a veneer of calm, but inside he felt anything but composed. A storm of emotions brewed beneath his carefully controlled expression as he maintained eye contact with John, unwilling to back down completely but equally unwilling to escalate the situation.

From across the bar, Lucy watched the interaction with growing anxiety, her senses heightened by the palpable tension. She kept a careful distance while remaining alert to any signs that the situation might deteriorate further. John's bravado felt threatening, sending ripples of uncertainty through the dingy room.

As the tension continued to rise, Lucy caught a glimpse of her reflection in a cracked mirror behind the bar. The glass fractured her image into disconnected pieces, a fitting metaphor for her own distorted self-perception shaped by trauma and psychosis. She looked away quickly, unwilling to confront that particular reality at this moment.

Larry suddenly interrupted the standoff, leaning on the bar with wide, dilated eyes, oblivious to the tension he was disrupting.

"Have you had your hit yet, Peter?" he asked excitedly, his voice a little too loud in the confined space. "Come on, mate! Join in on the fun!"

Peter, caught off guard by this shift in the atmosphere, swallowed hard. The stakes seemed to rise with each passing moment as the tension thickened, his eyes darting between Larry's manic expression and John's cold, evaluating stare.

Without warning, Larry entered the restroom again, his footsteps hurried. The sound of him searching the toilet cubicle echoed out to the bar. When he returned moments later, his demeanour had completely changed—his face flushed with anger, eyes bulging with rage.

"Who the fuck has taken my blow!?" he yelled, looking around accusingly.

The bar went silent, all eyes turning to Larry as he stormed around, fuming with indignation. Lucy's heart raced as she gripped the edge of the bar for support, but time seemed to slow around her. In that moment of heightened tension, her expression revealed a complex mixture of fear and unexpected bravery, a whirlwind of emotions washing across her face. Her gaze locked with Peter's across the room, a silent plea for connection in the midst of the chaos unfolding around them.

John stood up suddenly, his movement deliberate and threatening as he flexed his shoulders, a smug grin plastered across his face.

"What of it, you silly cunt?" he asked sarcastically, openly admitting to taking the drugs. "What you gonna do?"

The tension in the room hit a boiling point as Larry and John squared up to each other, shoulders hunched, testosterone and cocaine fuelling their aggression. The air felt electric with potential violence, emotions spiralling out of control in the confined space.

"You'd better step back, or you'll regret it," Larry barked, though he was clearly outmatched by John's more substantial frame and evident comfort with confrontation.

Lucy gripped the bar even tighter, her knuckles white with pressure as she watched the scene unfold. In that moment of potential violence, a strange thought crossed her mind—a moment of clarity amid the chaos.

'What about the violence that surrounds me? She wondered silently. Maybe they are just as broken as I am?'

The realization brought no comfort, only a deeper understanding of the damaged world she and Peter had escaped into—a world that might prove just as dangerous as the one they'd left behind, only in different ways. The broken mirror behind her showed not just her fractured reflection now, but the splintered reality of their new existence at The Trout Inn, surrounded by people carrying their own dangerous demons.

Peter felt a surge of helplessness. He couldn't call the police, not without risking exposure for both him and Lucy. They were trapped, forced to be passive observers in a drama that was rapidly escalating. He hated himself for his inaction, for his inability to protect Lucy from the violence that seemed to follow them like a curse. I'm a coward, he thought bitterly. I can't even protect the one person who actually needs me. He looked at Lucy, her eyes wide with fear, and a wave of self-loathing washed over him. He wished he could be someone else, someone stronger, someone capable of taking control of the situation. But all he could do was stand there, frozen in place, as the storm clouds gathered.

Lucy's mind raced, searching for a way out, a course of action. But her options were limited. She couldn't call the police, not without revealing her own past and inviting scrutiny that could tear apart the fragile life she was trying to build with Peter. And even if she could, would the police here be any different from the ones she had fled in London? Corrupt, indifferent, or simply outmatched by the forces at play in this forgotten corner of the country? She felt a familiar despair creeping in, the sense that she was trapped in a cycle of violence and helplessness from which there was no escape. 'Is this all I'm ever going to be? she wondered, her heart sinking. A victim, a bystander, a magnet for chaos?'

Chapter 24:
Blood on the Floor

With an impulsive charge born of cocaine-fuelled rage, Larry suddenly lunged at John, landing a punch that lacked real force—merely a weak attempt from a man unaccustomed to physical confrontation. The blow glanced off John's jaw, doing little but igniting his fury.

John retaliated immediately, striking Larry with several brutal blows that echoed through the small pub. The sickening sound of fist meeting flesh resonated in the room as Larry crashed to the floor, blood pouring from his mouth where a tooth had been dislodged by the impact.

John smirked, clearly taking pleasure in Larry's disarray as he leaned back against the bar, jaw flexed in triumph, his dominance established for all to see.

"You call that a hit?" he asked with a light laugh, looking down at Larry's crumpled form with contempt.

Peter and Lucy exchanged horrified glances across the bar, shock and disbelief evident on their faces. This was not the fresh start they had envisioned—this was a nightmare unfolding before their eyes, and they were trapped in the middle of it with no escape route.

Lucy watched, transfixed with horror, as Larry struggled to his feet. As Lucy watched on the scene warped. Everything slowed, the sounds of the bar fading into a muffled hum as the violence took centre stage. John's face morphed, his features contorting into a grotesque mask of cruelty. He wasn't just a man anymore, but a symbol of every bully, every abuser, every person who had ever made her feel small and worthless.

Though Larry was bruised and bloodied, his face was contorted with a rage that seemed to transcend his physical pain. With deliberate movements that sent chills down Lucy's spine, Larry picked up a pint glass from the bar and smashed it against the hard surface, shattering it into jagged pieces that scattered across the counter like the fragments of Peter and Lucy's shattered sense of safety.

Peter stood rooted behind the bar, body locked in place by a numb, involuntary paralysis. Around him, chaos exploded into motion—shouts, blood, the sickening sound of fists on flesh—but neither he nor Lucy moved, or spoke, or even seemed to breathe. He didn't run or cry out for help; he simply remained there, limbs heavy and useless, senses dulled, as if time itself had congealed and trapped him in its grip. Only after the violence had ended did the world seem to unfreeze, and his body slowly, painfully, remembered how to move. The violence was not over yet, though.

With a quick motion that no one anticipated, Larry grabbed one of the larger shards of glass, gripping it tightly despite the way it cut into his own palm. Anger fuelled his next move as he lunged toward John from behind, catching him off-guard as he turned away to take a smug sip of his beer.

In Lucy's mind, the scene warped. Everything slowed, the sounds of the bar fading into a muffled hum as the violence took centre stage. John's face morphed, his features contorting into a grotesque mask of cruelty. He wasn't just a man anymore, but a symbol of every bully, every abuser, every person who had ever made her feel small and worthless.

Jim's voice whispered in her ear, a seductive invitation: "Do it, Lucy. End him. Show them what you're capable of.

In a split second that seemed to stretch into eternity, Larry plunged the glass shard deep into John's neck with savage force. Blood immediately sprayed across the bar in a crimson arc, spattering the counter, the floor, and the horrified patrons who hadn't moved quickly enough to avoid it. Cries of panic erupted from around the room as people scrambled away from the violence.

The world around Peter and Lucy seemed to spin into chaos, reality taking on a surreal quality as they witnessed the brutality unfold before them. Lucy covered her mouth with both hands, fighting back tears as terror set in, cementing her to the spot behind the bar.

A part of her was horrified, disgusted by the violence, desperate to stop it, to rewind time and prevent it from ever happening. But another part—a darker, more primal part—was strangely fascinated, almost aroused by the raw display of power and rage. The line between victim and perpetrator, between right and wrong, blurred until it disappeared entirely.

"What the fuck...?" John choked out, his words gargled with the blood filling his throat, his eyes wide with the realization of his own mortality.

His body faltered, beginning to collapse, but Larry wasn't finished. With a savagery that seemed to come from somewhere beyond rational thought, Larry shoved the same glass shard into John's eye. A sickening squelch filled the air as the makeshift weapon penetrated, the sound somehow worse than the visual horror, further staining the floor with fresh crimson that pooled around their feet.

Chaos erupted. Lucy remained frozen, her world spiralling beyond control. The stripper screamed, frantically trying to find cover behind the bar, clutching at her discarded clothes as she moved. In stark contrast, the elderly local—the same man who had been there when they arrived—simply sat back down at his usual spot, seemingly unfazed by the violence as he casually sipped his drink.

Larry, now completely consumed by a primal fury that had overtaken any semblance of humanity, grabbed a black pool ball from the nearby table, his blood-slicked fingers leaving red smears on its surface.

"You fat cunt—this is what happens!" he snarled, breathing heavily, his rage transcending rational thought as he towered over John's faltering form.

With devastating force, he brought the pool ball down on John's head repeatedly, the sickening sound of impact echoing against the horrified silence from the others around them. Each blow landed with a terrible finality, turning John's features into an unrecognizable mask of blood and tissue.

"Peter! What's happening!?" Lucy cried out, her voice breaking with terror as she reached for him across the bar, desperate for some anchor in the storm of violence that had erupted around them.

Peter stood frozen beside her, his heart pounding so loudly he was sure everyone could hear it, a mixture of horror and disbelief washing over his features. He couldn't move, couldn't speak, and couldn't process the brutality unfolding before him — far worse than anything he had imagined encountering in this remote seaside town.

As the brutal assault continued beyond what seemed possible, Larry finally stepped back, his energy spent. John's lifeless body lay sprawled on the floor, blood pooling around him in an ever-widening circle that seemed to reach toward Lucy and Peter like grasping fingers.

Peter turned to Lucy, their shared sense of dread amplifying as silence descended upon the pub—the chaotic past they had fled morphing into something darker, something they could no longer ignore or escape. They had witnessed a murder, and there was no going back from that knowledge.

The ruckus finally settled into an uncomfortable silence, leaving Peter and Lucy in stark contrast to the violent scene that had just unfolded. Lucy turned away from John's body on the floor, breathing heavily as she tried to process what she had witnessed. Their hearts raced in terrified unison, every beat audible in the eerie quiet that had fallen over the pub.

Each breath sounded thunderous in the silence, the normal ambient noises of the establishment suspended in the aftermath of shocking violence. Finally, the silence was broken as Larry glanced at Peter, a casual smile forming on his blood-spattered face as if nothing out of the ordinary had happened.

"Fancy that line now, yeah?" he asked, grinning in a way that suggested the murder he had just committed was no more significant than ordering another drink.

As if shifting back to normal reality while everyone else remained frozen in shock, Larry strolled into the restroom, leaving Peter and Lucy to grapple with what they had just witnessed. An overwhelming weight of reality crashed down around them, suffocating in its intensity.

Peter and Lucy exchanged horrified glances, unsure of what to say or do next as they confronted the consequences of their decision to come to this place—their fleeting sense of safety now completely shattered. The terror on their faces mirrored each other, a reflection of the tension that bound them together in this shared nightmare.

They had escaped one dangerous situation only to find themselves witness to something far worse, caught in a web of violence and criminality that threatened to entangle them completely. The chaos they had just witnessed felt like a twisted reflection of their own entangled lives—the nightmarish new world they had willingly entered in search of refuge proving to be no sanctuary at all.

Chapter 25:
Exposure

Night had fallen completely, shrouding the world in darkness. In a dimly lit room somewhere far from The Trout Inn, shadows crept against walls as if they were living things, stretching and contracting with subtle movements. A man sat hunched over a desk, his form illuminated solely by the faint blue-white glow of a laptop screen. His face remained shrouded in obscurity, the contours of his features concealed by the darkness that enveloped everything beyond the computer's harsh light.

The screen displayed a web browser unlike those used by ordinary internet users. This was the dark web—a hidden corner of the internet where anonymity reigned and the darkest aspects of humanity found expression. Numerous tabs lined the top of the browser, each containing content rendered in incomprehensible symbols and flickering images that would disturb most who glimpsed them.

The man's hands moved with practiced precision across the keyboard, the reflection of the screen's luminescent light dancing across his pale skin, highlighting every vein and tendon. As he navigated through pages, the sound of clacking keys filled the air—a mundane yet somehow invasive sound in the silent void of the room. Each keystroke seemed to punctuate the darkness, like Morse code transmitting his depravity into the void.

He paused, the cursor hovering over the search bar. The soft light from the screen illuminated enough of his lower body to reveal his trousers bunched around his ankles—a stark hint of the perversion that lurked behind his mundane facade. A murmur of trepidation filled the air, as if the room itself held its breath in anticipation of what would come next.

With a single click, he typed in "CCTV footage homeless massacre" and pressed Enter. The screen flickered momentarily, betraying the depth of his search as various algorithms parsed his request, searching through repositories of content never meant for public consumption.

The results loaded quickly, a series of video thumbnails spilling across the screen, each depicting grotesque events that would sicken ordinary people. But this man was not ordinary—his interest in these horrors went beyond mere curiosity. One video in particular stood out among the others, its title inscribed brightly against the dark background: "CCTV footage of homeless massacre, schizophrenic bludgeoning."

The man's breathing quickened noticeably, a mixture of intrigue and something darker, more primal, as he moved the cursor toward the video. With a sharp click that seemed to echo in the empty room, he selected it.

The screen changed, displaying a grainy black and white CCTV recording. The footage was shot from a high angle, the camera positioned far away, capturing a late-night scene in what appeared to be an alleyway. Despite the poor quality and distant perspective, the content was unmistakable—a chaotic exchange between two figures, one of whom was attacking the other with shocking violence.

This was Lucy, though no viewer could possibly know her name from this anonymous footage. Her identity was further obscured by the hoodie she wore, casting her face in shadow. Yet even from this distance, even though the grainy footage, the brutality of the scene was evident as she repeatedly struck the homeless man with the brick.

The man watching leaned closer to the screen, his eyes never blinking, absorbing every pixel of the violence with disturbing attention. His fingers moved again, pressing a few buttons to enhance the footage. The screen shifted from the grainy, distant image to a crisper, nearly 4K resolution—clearly enhanced using sophisticated software. Now every detail became visible: the wild terror in Lucy's eyes during the brief moments her face was captured by the camera, the darkness that seemed to envelop her as she swung the brick again and again.

The enhanced footage revealed an intimate, visceral reality that the original recording had only hinted at. The man's breathing grew more ragged as he leaned ever closer, his fingers grazing the keyboard as the atmosphere in the room thickened with tension and unspoken desire.

As the enhanced footage played, somewhere far from London, a set of eyes watched intently, a knowing smile spreading across a face that was itself reflected in a bank of similar CCTV screens.

The video played to its conclusion, showing Lucy fleeing the scene, leaving behind the broken body of the homeless man. As the footage ended, the man's silhouette lingered in the blue glow of the screen—an ominous reflection of his depravity as he sat motionless, entranced by the hand of fate that had played out before him and, more significantly, by the woman at the centre of the violence.

In the silence that followed, one thing became clear through the darkness: Lucy's secret was no longer hers alone. Someone was watching. Someone knew what she had done. And that someone had plans of his own.

The chilling events captured in that footage continued to exist in the digital world, setting the stage for what was to come—echoing the intertwining lives of those marked by chaos, despair, and the burden of their secrets.

On the table next to the laptop was a simple, black text on a glossy white business card: "Mercer Environmental Solutions - Discreet Waste Management Services."

Chapter 26:
Aftermath

Back at The Trout Inn, the aftermath of violence lingered in the air, heavy and unsettling. Larry and the old man walked out of the pub as if nothing unusual had happened, leaving Peter and Lucy behind with their minds swirling with memories of what they had witnessed. The bar door swung shut behind them with a soft thud, sealing in the tension that remained.

Lucy's mind replayed the gruesome scene: the sound of fist on flesh, the shattering glass, the blood spraying across the room. She couldn't shake the image of John's lifeless eyes staring up at the ceiling. Had this been the right escape?

Peter and Lucy stood frozen behind the bar, locked in a moment of shared shock. The world outside seemed to fade away—the clinking of glass and the low murmur of the few remaining patrons dimming into the background as their own heartbeats thundered in their ears.

Peter felt a profound sense of despair settling over him. 'This is it,' he thought. 'This is how it ends. Not with a bang, but with a whimper. In some shithole pub, surrounded by violence and decay.' He looked at Lucy, her face blank with shock, and a wave of anger washed over him. 'Why have I dragged us here, am I destroying my entire life just because I have a pathetic yearning for connection?' he thought. 'She still deserves better than this, and I've dragged her into this mess.' He clenched his fists, his jaw tight with determination. 'I have to get her out of here,' he thought. 'I have to find a way to protect her, even if it means leaving my hopes of a life behind.' The thought was agonizing, but he knew it might be the only way to save her. 'I can't drag her down with me,' he thought.

Their bodies remained tense, hearts racing from the adrenaline of the earlier violence. The flickering fluorescent lights above cast ghostly shadows across their faces, highlighting the strain of their shared trauma. From somewhere in the corner, a somber song about society's outcasts played softly from the pub's ancient jukebox, its haunting melody resonating with the despair and stark reality of their situation.

Peter's hands trembled as he reached for a glass to wipe down. He wasn't sure what to do. What were they going to do? He almost wished he had never met Lucy. What was wrong with them to witness this?

The atmosphere was thick with unspoken words, an overwhelming vulnerability wrapping around them like a shroud. Peter bit his lip, his fingers twitching nervously at the edge of the bar as he struggled to process what he had witnessed. Lucy fidgeted with her hands, her pulse racing as her breathing became increasingly shallow.

'We're trapped,' Lucy thought. 'We have to get out of here. But where can we go? We cannot trust anyone.'

For a heartbeat, time seemed to stretch infinitely, and the night weighed heavy on their shoulders. They could feel the adrenaline still coursing through their veins long after the actual violence had ended, keeping them in a state of hyperawareness that was both exhausting and impossible to escape.

'I should have done something,' Peter thought, guilt washing over him. 'I should have stopped it. What good is it to run if we still end up in places like this?'

Lucy stared blankly at the stained floor, her mind racing back to the horrific scene, replaying it in vivid flashes—John's lifeless body sprawled across the bar, blood pooling around him in a crimson lake that seemed to grow with each passing second. She swallowed hard, feeling the warmth of bile rise in her throat. Peter stood beside her, his knuckles white as he gripped the edge of the bar, trembling under the weight of unprocessed emotions.

'How could I be so stupid?' Lucy thought. 'How could I let myself get into this situation? I want to go home. No, I don't have a home anymore.'

Peter glanced at Lucy out of the corner of his eye, sensing her fear. His heart pounded in his chest as he reflexively shuffled closer to her, an unspoken gesture of solidarity amidst the horror that had unfolded before them. They had both chosen this place, this escape, and now they were bound by the shared knowledge of a murder.

They both remained silent, the gravity of the situation pressing down like a suffocating blanket. The tune from the jukebox continued to weave through the silence, intertwining its melody with the weight of their current plight. Jim's voice echoed in Lucy's ears, a constant reminder of her fractured state: 'See, Lucy? This is what you attract. You can't escape it.'

Lucy's hands shook as she absently fiddled with the hem of her shirt. The weight of guilt and the trauma of witnessing such brutality clawed at her insides, yet she couldn't bring herself to voice the turmoil bubbling beneath the surface. There were no words adequate for the horror they had just experienced.

Peter watched Lucy closely, noting her face—pale and drawn, the shadows circling her eyes revealing her emotional exhaustion. His heart ached for her, a mix of protective instincts surfacing along with frustration at his own inaction during the violence. He had frozen, they both had, and that knowledge sat heavily between them.

His breath quickened as he felt the buildup of anxiety but couldn't find the words to express it. Instead, he reached for her hand, their fingers tenderly intertwining, silently promising they were in this together, even as the terrible weight of the incident loomed over them.

In Lucy's mind, Jim's laughter echoed, unsettling and dark, spiralling further into the depths of her inner turmoil. Even amidst this real-world violence, her hallucinations remained present, blurring the line between external dangers and internal demons.

The room felt claustrophobic, shadows closing in as Peter glanced at Lucy, her eyes wide with disbelief. The atmosphere grew heavy, her heart racing. She looked fragile and small in this harsh environment, her body trembling slightly as her mind raced through possibilities, consequences, and escapes.

Peter's breath caught in his throat, the emotional weight of the night settling heavily on him. He instinctively tightened his grip on Lucy's hand, an attempt at reassurance, but the uncertainty in her eyes made his heart ache with the knowledge that he could offer no real protection in this world they had entered.

The atmosphere pulsed with lingering shock, and the silence between them amplified their fear. The only sound beyond the music was the faint dripping of a nearby tap, each drop echoing like a time bomb in their minds.

The walls seemed to close in around them as they both reflected on the traumatic event they had just witnessed—a spectral reminder of their own vulnerability in a world where violence could erupt without warning.

A moment stretched into what felt like eternity before the landlord stormed back into the bar, an expression of apoplectic fury plastered across his weathered face.

"What the fuck happened in here?" he shouted, his voice low and threatening despite its volume. "Why the hell didn't you clean up the mess?"

His eyes darted between Peter and Lucy hungrily, seeking someone to blame. Catching his breath, he scanned the bar floor where John's blood still pooled, a mix of anger and disbelief boiling within him.

Lucy glanced at Peter, both feeling a sense of cowardice wash over them as they struggled to confront their own inaction. They stood awkwardly, mouths slightly parted but no words emerging, the weight of the landlord's fury hanging over them like an executioner's axe.

The landlord's frustration flared visibly, his expression oscillating between rage and something that might have been fear as he laced into them.

"You two are fucking useless cunts!" he spat, spraying saliva with the force of his words. "I'll take care of this myself! Just fuck off, and we'll talk about this later!"

Lucy and Peter shifted awkwardly, guilt pooling in their stomachs as they avoided the landlord's accusatory gaze. Both felt a twinge of shame wash over them, their previous determination dissipating in the face of this confrontation. Lucy looked down at her feet, her heart racing as the gravity of their situation sank in further.

The landlord strode away from them with disgust, pulling out his phone as he continued muttering under his breath. His fingers jabbed at the screen with practiced precision as he dialled what seemed to be some kind of clean-up crew, not bothering to acknowledge Peter and

Lucy any further. His manner suggested this wasn't the first time he'd had to orchestrate such a cleanup—his irritation reflected a pattern, a cycle of violence deeply embedded in this hellhole of a pub.

"Yeah, it's me," they heard him say gruffly into the phone as he disappeared into the back room. "We've got another situation. Same as before... Yeah, tonight. Now."

The casual way he spoke about arranging the disposal of a dead body sent chills down Lucy's spine. This place was far more dangerous than they had initially realized, a realization that came too late.

Lucy and Peter exchanged looks, their bodies visibly shaking as the violent upheaval of the evening settled into their bones. Without speaking, they made a silent agreement to retreat to their room. They moved quietly, avoiding the bloodstained area of the floor, slipping away before the landlord returned.

Their shared room felt even smaller and more oppressive than before. The initial excitement of having found shelter and work had completely dissipated, replaced by a deep, gnawing dread now that they were alone again with the knowledge of what they had witnessed.

Lucy sat on the edge of the thin mattress, her hair falling forward to obscure her face as she stared at her trembling hands. "We can't stay here," she whispered, her voice barely audible over the distant sounds of the pub below.

Peter paced the small space, running his fingers through his hair repeatedly. "I know," he agreed, "but where else can we go? We've got no money, no connections... nothing."

The grim reality of their situation hung in the air between them. They had fled one dangerous situation only to find themselves in one potentially worse—witnesses to a murder in a place where such violence seemed routine.

"We need to sleep," Peter finally said, his voice heavy with exhaustion. "We can figure it out in the morning."

Lucy nodded numbly, though sleep seemed impossible with the images of violence still fresh in her mind. Nevertheless, they both lay down on the thin mattress, fully clothed, their bodies instinctively curling toward each other for comfort in the darkness

CHAPTER 27:
AN UNEXPECTED OPPORTUNITY

The morning arrived with grey light filtering through the grimy window of their room. Lucy awoke first, momentarily disoriented before the memories of the previous night came flooding back. Peter slept beside her, his face relaxed in sleep in a way it never was when he was awake.

For a few minutes, she simply watched him breathe, finding a strange comfort in the rhythm of his chest rising and falling. Despite everything, despite the horror they had witnessed and the precariousness of their situation, she felt a connection to him that she couldn't explain—as if fate had deliberately thrown them together for some purpose neither of them yet understood.

A sharp knock at the door jolted her from these thoughts. Peter woke with a start, sitting up quickly, eyes wide with alarm.

"Who is it?" Lucy called, her voice trembling slightly.

"Landlord," came the gruff reply. "Get decent and come downstairs. Someone's here to see you both."

Before either of them could respond, they heard his heavy footsteps retreating down the hallway.

"Someone to see us?" Peter whispered, confusion evident in his expression. "Who would be looking for us here?"

Lucy shook her head, equally perplexed. "I don't know. Maybe it's the police?" The thought sent a fresh wave of panic through her.

"If it was the police, they'd have broken down the door," Peter reasoned, though he didn't sound entirely convinced. "Let's just go down and see."

They made themselves as presentable as possible given the circumstances—splashing water on their faces, Lucy combing her fingers through her hair, Peter straightening his rumpled clothes. Neither spoke much, the tension between them building with each passing moment.

When they descended the narrow staircase to the pub below, they found it eerily clean. No trace remained of the violence that had occurred the night before—the blood had been scrubbed away, furniture rearranged, surfaces polished to a dull shine. It was as if the murder had never happened.

Standing at the bar was a man they had never seen before. He was tall and immaculately dressed in a tailored suit that seemed wildly out of place in the dingy surroundings of The Trout Inn. His face was handsome in a conventional way, with sharp features and eyes that seemed to miss nothing. He turned as they approached, a smile spreading across his face that didn't quite reach those watchful eyes.

"Ah, you must be Peter and Lucy," he said, his voice smooth and cultured. "I've been looking forward to meeting you."

Lucy felt a chill run down her spine, though she couldn't have explained why. There was something familiar about this man, something unsettling that she couldn't quite place.

"Who are you?" Peter asked bluntly, positioning himself slightly in front of Lucy in an unconsciously protective gesture.

"My name is David Mercer," the man replied, extending a hand that neither Lucy nor Peter moved to take. He withdrew it gracefully, seemingly unbothered by their wariness. "I own a hotel about twenty miles from here. The Ornate Sapphire. Perhaps you've heard of it?"

What if the landlord at the Trout Inn was hired by David, and he was waiting for them all along? He did seem to be very calm given the circumstances. Lucy could not rid herself of the thought that this was too good to be true. A shiver ran down her spine.

They both shook their heads.

"No matter," David continued. "I understand you're looking for work, and as it happens, I'm in need of staff. The landlord here—an old friend of mine—mentioned you'd arrived recently."

He gestured toward the landlord, who stood behind the bar watching the exchange with an unreadable expression.

"I'm offering you both positions at my hotel," David explained. "Full accommodation included, of course. Better quarters than what you have here, I can assure you." His eyes briefly took in their dishevelled appearance with what might have been pity.

Lucy and Peter exchanged glances, confusion and wary hope mingling in their expressions. This seemed too convenient, too perfect a solution to their immediate problems.

"Why us?" Lucy asked, unable to keep the suspicion from her voice. "You don't know anything about us."

David's smile widened slightly. "On the contrary, I know you're both hard workers who aren't afraid of... unusual situations. That's exactly the kind of staff I need."

The implication hung in the air—he knew what had happened last night, knew they had witnessed a murder and said nothing. This knowledge could be held over them, but it was also being presented as a qualification for the job he was offering.

"The Ornate is a special place," David continued when neither of them immediately responded. "Secluded, peaceful. A place where people can... start fresh." His eyes lingered on Lucy's new haircut, a visible symbol of her attempt at transformation. "I think you'll find it's exactly what you've been looking for."

Lucy felt Peter tense beside her, clearly as uncertain about this proposition as she was. But what choice did they have? They couldn't stay at The Trout Inn, not after what had happened. And they had nowhere else to go, no money, and no other prospects.

"When would we start?" Peter asked after a moment, his voice carefully neutral.

"Today," David replied without hesitation. "I have a car waiting outside."

Another exchanged glance between Lucy and Peter, a silent communication passing between them. Despite the strangeness of the offer, despite the lingering suspicion, they both recognized this for what it was—an escape. And that was what they needed more than anything.

"Alright," Lucy said finally, speaking for both of them. "We'll come."

David's smile broadened, a flash of something like triumph passing across his features before it was carefully masked. "Excellent. Gather your things. We'll leave within the hour."

As Lucy and Peter turned to go back upstairs for their meagre belongings, Lucy couldn't shake the feeling that they were trading one dangerous situation for another. Yet there was something else too—a strange sense of inevitability, as if they were being drawn along a path that had been laid out for them long ago.

'Just get through today', she told herself. 'One day at a time.'

But deep in her mind, in a place not yet touched by the medication that still dulled Jim's voice, something whispered that time was running out. The path they were on was leading somewhere dark, somewhere from which there might be no return.

She pushed the thought away, following Peter up the stairs, clinging to the thin hope that this unexpected opportunity might be the salvation they both desperately needed.

Chapter 28:
THE ORNATE SAPPHIRE

The journey to The Ornate Sapphire Hotel took place in near-complete silence. David drove a sleek black Audi that seemed impossibly clean given the muddy country roads they traversed. Lucy and Peter sat in the back seat, their few belongings in a small bag between them, shoulders occasionally touching as the car navigated winding roads that took them deeper into isolation.

David kept his eyes fixed on the road, his grip tight on the steering wheel. The air conditioning hummed softly, hissing almost, maintaining a constant, almost unnerving temperature.

Through the window, Lucy watched the landscape change—becoming more rugged, more remote with each passing mile. The seaside town faded into the distance, and with it, the immediate horror of what they had witnessed at The Trout Inn. Yet the memory remained, burned into her consciousness, impossible to escape completely.

"The Ornate Sapphire has been in my family for generations," David said, breaking the silence as they rounded a curve and the hotel came into view. "We've maintained its... unique character over the years."

The building stood alone on a hillside, a grand Victorian structure that seemed to both belong to the landscape and stand apart from it. Its imposing facade featured large windows that reflected the grey sky, giving the impression that the building was watching their approach with dozens of glassy eyes.

"It's beautiful," Lucy murmured, though beautiful wasn't quite the right word. Striking, perhaps. Commanding. There was something almost hypnotic about the way the building dominated the horizon.

"It has a certain presence," David agreed, a note of pride in his voice. "Most of our guests come for extended stays. They find the isolation... therapeutic."

Peter shifted uneasily in his seat, a prickling sensation crawling across his skin. The car crunched to a stop on the gravel driveway. Up close, the hotel revealed signs of age that hadn't been visible from a distance—peeling paint in places, a slight sag to the front steps, ivy creeping up one wall in a way that suggested years of unrestricted growth. Yet these imperfections only added to its character, giving it a lived-in feeling that was somehow both welcoming and slightly unsettling.

"Come," David said, leading them inside. "I'll show you to your quarters first, then we can discuss your duties."

The interior of The Ornate Sapphire was a study in faded grandeur—high ceilings, ornate woodwork, plush carpets worn thin in places by years of footsteps. The air smelled of furniture polish and something else, something older and more difficult to identify. Despite the numerous windows, the interior remained dim, as if the building itself preferred shadows to light.

Lucy couldn't shake the feeling that she was being watched, that every corner held a pair of eyes observing their every move. *I need to be careful. This isn't over. Not by a long shot.* Despite her apprehension and obvious distrust, they didn't have anywhere else to go and Lucy didn't trust her own instincts at this point.

Their room—a staff accommodation on the hotel's third floor—was spacious and clean, far more comfortable than the squalid space they'd occupied at The Trout Inn. A large bed dominated the room, covered in a quilt that looked handmade. A wardrobe stood against one wall, a small desk and chair against another. The bathroom, though dated, was spotlessly clean, with fluffy white towels neatly folded on a shelf.

"I hope this will be suitable," David said, watching their reactions closely. "The staff quarters were refurbished last year."

"It's... more than suitable," Peter replied, unable to hide his surprise at the quality of the accommodation. "Thank you."

"Get settled in," David told them. "Rest if you need to. I'll be in my office when you're ready to discuss your responsibilities. First floor, end of the hall. No rush." He smiled again, that same smile that never quite reached his eyes, before closing the door softly behind him.

As soon as they were alone, Peter turned to Lucy. "What do you think?" he asked in a low voice, as if concerned they might be overheard. Lucy shivered, despite the warmth of the room

Lucy sat on the edge of the bed, running her hand over the quilt. "It seems too good to be true," she admitted. "Why would he offer us this? He doesn't know us."

"Maybe he really does need staff," Peter suggested, though he didn't sound convinced. "The place is huge. I haven't seen anyone else around."

"It's off-season, I guess," Lucy said. "But still..." She trailed off, unable to articulate exactly what was bothering her. Goosebumps ran up Lucys arm, a cold sweat across her forehead.

Peter sat beside her, their shoulders touching. "We can always leave if it doesn't feel right," he said, though they both knew that wasn't entirely true. They had nowhere else to go, no money, no resources beyond what David Mercer was offering them.

"Let's just... take it one day at a time," Lucy suggested, echoing her earlier thought. "See what he wants us to do, get our bearings. Maybe it'll be okay."

Peter nodded, taking her hand in his. "Maybe it will."

For a moment, they sat in silence, the weight of everything they had been through pressing down on them. The murder at The Trout Inn, their hasty departure, this strange new situation—it was almost too much to process. Yet here, in this clean, quiet room, with Peter's hand warm in hers, Lucy felt something she hadn't experienced in a long time: hope. Fragile and tentative, but hope nonetheless.

"I should take my medication," she said after a while, reaching for her bag. The routine had become important to her—a way of maintaining control, of keeping the voices at bay. She hadn't heard Jim since leaving The Trout Inn, and she wanted to keep it that way.

While she took her pill, Peter explored the room more thoroughly, opening drawers, checking the view from the windows. "It really is isolated here," he commented, peering out at the expanse of moor that surrounded the hotel. "Can't see another building for miles."

"Perfect place to hide," Lucy murmured, coming to stand beside him. The view was breathtaking in its starkness—rolling hills stretching to the horizon, the occasional stand of trees breaking the monotony, clouds casting moving shadows across the landscape. It felt like they were at the edge of the world.

"Or to be hidden," Peter added softly, a note of unease in his voice.

Lucy felt a shiver run down her spine at his words. She pushed the feeling away, focusing instead on the immediate future. "We should go find David," she said. "Find out what he expects us to do."

Peter nodded, and together they left the room, closing the door behind them. The corridor outside was long and lined with identical doors—other staff quarters, presumably, though they had yet to see evidence of other employees. Their footsteps were muffled by the threadbare carpet as they made their way toward the stairs.

The Ornate Sapphire seemed larger inside than it had appeared from the outside, its corridors twisting and turning in ways that defied Lucy's attempts to create a mental map. By the time they reached the first floor, she was thoroughly disoriented, relying entirely on Peter's apparently better sense of direction.

They found David's office exactly where he had said it would be—at the end of a hallway on the first floor. The door was partially open, warm light spilling out into the dimmer corridor. Peter knocked softly, and David's voice immediately called for them to enter.

The office was a stark contrast to the faded elegance of the rest of the hotel. Here, everything was modern, sleek, and meticulously organized. A large desk dominated the space, its surface clear except for a laptop and a single folder. Bookshelves lined one wall, filled with volumes that looked more decorative than well-read. The opposite wall featured a large window overlooking the same moorland view they had seen from their room, though from this vantage point, the landscape appeared even more vast and empty.

David himself sat behind the desk, his posture relaxed yet somehow still commanding. He gestured for them to take the two chairs positioned in front of the desk.

"I hope the accommodations meet with your approval," he said as they sat. "You'll find The Ornate offers certain... comforts that were lacking at your previous establishment."

"It's very nice," Lucy said cautiously. "We're grateful for the opportunity."

David smiled, that same unsettling smile that never quite reached his eyes. "I believe in giving people second chances, Lucy. Sometimes third or fourth chances." He paused, his gaze lingering on her face. "We all have pasts we'd rather leave behind, don't we?"

There was something in the way he said it that made Lucy's breath catch in her throat. Did he know? How could he? There was something about David's gaze that set Lucy on edge—a cold precision, as if he could see straight through her. She felt suddenly transparent, as if her secrets were hovering just beneath her skin, visible to anyone who cared to look hard enough. But that was impossible. David couldn't know what she had done. No one could. Still, the shiver of suspicion wouldn't leave her as she listened to him speak, each word tightening the knot of dread in her chest.

"What exactly will we be doing here?" Peter asked, his tone carefully neutral, drawing David's attention away from Lucy.

"Ah, yes. Your duties." David leaned back in his chair. "They're quite straightforward. The hotel is operating at reduced capacity at the moment—off-season, as you might expect. We have only a handful of guests, all long-term residents. Your responsibilities will be to maintain the public areas, assist with meal service, and generally ensure our guests have everything they need for a comfortable stay."

He opened the folder on his desk, removing two sheets of paper and sliding them across the surface. "Your daily schedules. You'll work together for the most part, but there are a few tasks that require individual attention."

Lucy glanced down at the paper, scanning the list of duties. Nothing seemed unusual or concerning—cleaning, serving meals, basic maintenance. The hours were reasonable, with adequate breaks. It all appeared perfectly normal, which somehow made her even more suspicious.

"And the other staff?" Peter asked, looking up from his own schedule. "We haven't seen anyone else."

"We operate with minimal personnel during the off-season," David explained smoothly. "There's a cook who comes in daily to prepare meals, and I handle the administrative aspects myself. You two will complete our little team quite nicely."

He stood suddenly, indicating the meeting was coming to an end. "You'll start tomorrow morning. Today, feel free to familiarize yourselves with the hotel. Explore, get your bearings. Dinner is served in the main dining room at seven. You'll meet our guests then."

With that, they were dismissed, ushered back into the corridor with their schedules in hand. The door closed behind them with a soft click that somehow sounded very final.

As they walked away, Lucy noticed a faint scent lingering in the air—something like ozone, with a metallic undertone. It was the scent of a room that was constantly being cleaned, sterilized, and monitored.

"Well," Peter said as they walked away, "that was..."

"Strange," Lucy finished for him. "The whole thing is strange. Don't you think it's weird that there are 'long-term residents' here? Who stays at a hotel in the middle of nowhere for long periods?"

Peter shrugged, though his expression suggested he shared her concerns. "People with money and secrets, I guess. Same as us, but with the money part."

Lucy couldn't argue with that logic. They were hardly in a position to question the motivations of others, given their own circumstances. Lucy glanced around the hallway, its marble floors polished to a mirror's shine, chandeliers burning too brightly overhead. The air was thick with perfume and something else she couldn't name—a metallic tang that lingered at the back of her throat. She tried to ignore the way every surface seemed to reflect her face back at odd angles, stretching her features, making her feel smaller than she was.

"Let's explore," she suggested, pushing her unease aside. "Like he said, get our bearings. I already feel like I could get lost in here."

Peter nodded, glancing up at a painting that hung just a little too high on the wall. Together, they wandered the corridors, their footsteps muffled by thick carpet. Mirrors caught their movements, glinting in the corners of her eyes. Somewhere, a door clicked shut; Lucy couldn't tell from where. The hallway seemed to curve in on itself, leading them past empty armchairs and closed doors that whispered as they passed. She couldn't shake the sense that they were being drawn forward, step by step, as if the hotel itself had been waiting for them.

Chapter 29:
The Residents

The Ornate Sapphire revealed itself gradually as Lucy and Peter explored its labyrinthine corridors. The hotel was larger than it had first appeared, with numerous wings and extensions that seemed to have been added haphazardly over decades, creating a confusing layout that defied logical navigation. Some areas were meticulously maintained, while others showed signs of neglect—dusty corners, water stains on the ceiling, doors that appeared to have been sealed shut for years.

"I feel like we're walking through different time periods," Lucy commented as they moved from a newly renovated section into a corridor that looked like it hadn't been updated since the 1970s. "It's like the place can't decide what it wants to be."

"Or who it wants to remember," Peter added, pausing to examine a wall of framed photographs. The images chronicled the hotel's history—black and white photos from its grand opening, colour snapshots of notable guests over the years, group photos of staff standing in neat rows on the front steps.

Lucy joined him, studying the faces captured in the photographs. Something about one particular group photo caught her attention—a staff photo that appeared to be from the 1990s based on the fashion and hairstyles. She leaned closer, her breath catching in her throat.

"Peter," she whispered, pointing to a figure standing in the back row. "Does that look like...?"

Peter followed her gaze, his eyes widening slightly. "David," he confirmed. "But that's impossible. He'd have been a child back then."

The man in the photograph was indeed the spitting image of David Mercer—the same sharp features, the same calculating eyes. The only difference was the style of clothing and the slightly longer hair.

"Maybe it's his father?" Lucy suggested, though she didn't sound convinced. There was something unsettling about the resemblance, about the way the man in the photograph seemed to be looking directly at the camera as if he knew, decades in advance, that they would be standing here now, examining his image.

"Probably," Peter agreed, a note of uncertainty in his voice. "Family business, like he said."

They continued their exploration, eventually finding their way to the main lobby—a grand space with a high ceiling, ornate chandelier, and wide staircase leading to the upper floors. The reception desk stood empty; a small bell placed precisely in its centre. Beyond the lobby was a lounge area with comfortable-looking sofas and armchairs arranged around a massive stone fireplace.

"I wonder where all the guests are," Lucy mused, noting the emptiness of the common areas. "David said there were long-term residents, but we haven't seen anyone."

"Maybe they keep to themselves," Peter suggested. "If I was staying in a place this isolated, I'd probably want privacy too."

As if summoned by their conversation, a door at the far end of the lounge opened, and a woman stepped through. She was in her sixties, elegantly dressed in a style that seemed from another era—a tweed skirt suit, pearls at her throat, her silver hair perfectly styled. She paused when she saw them, a look of surprise crossing her features before it was quickly replaced with a polite smile.

"You must be the new staff," she said, approaching them with an extended hand. "I'm Margaret Ellison. I've been a resident here for... oh, longer than I care to admit."

Lucy shook the woman's hand, noting the coolness of her skin and the strength of her grip. "Lucy," she introduced herself. "And this is Peter."

"A pleasure," Margaret said, turning her attention to Peter. "David mentioned he was bringing in some new blood. The place has been dreadfully understaffed lately."

Something about the phrase "new blood" sent a shiver down Lucy's spine, though she couldn't explain why. Margaret seemed perfectly pleasant, if a bit formal in her manner.

"Have you been shown around properly?" Margaret asked, looking between them. "The Ornate Sapphire can be quite confusing for newcomers. So many additions over the years, you see. The original structure dates back to 1878, but the east wing wasn't added until 1923, and then the west extension came along in the fifties..."

She continued chatting about the hotel's architectural history as she led them on an impromptu tour, pointing out features they had missed in their earlier exploration. Lucy noted how confidently Margaret navigated the confusing layout, turning corners without hesitation, and unlocking doors with keys she produced from a pocket in her skirt.

"And this," Margaret said eventually, stopping before a set of double doors, "is the dining room. Where you'll be serving this evening, I understand."

She pushed the doors open to reveal a grand dining room that could easily seat fifty people, though only one long table in the centre was set for a meal. Crystal chandeliers hung from the ceiling, their light reflecting off the polished silver and glassware on the table.

"There are only six of us at present," Margaret explained, noting their surprise at the small number of place settings. "All long-term guests. We dine together each evening at seven sharp. David insists on maintaining certain... traditions."

"How long have you all been staying here?" Peter asked, his curiosity getting the better of him.

A shadow seemed to pass over Margaret's face, though her smile remained fixed in place. "Oh, we all have our stories," she said vaguely. "Some of us have been here for years, some more recently. The Ornate Sapphire provides a certain sanctuary, you see. A place apart from the world and its... judgments."

Before either Lucy or Peter could ask for clarification, the dining room doors opened again, and David Mercer entered. He looked momentarily surprised to find them there with Margaret, but quickly recovered.

"I see you've met Mrs. Ellison," he said smoothly. "I hope she's been enlightening you about our little establishment."

"Just giving them a proper tour," Margaret replied. "Something you should have done yourself, David."

There was a familiarity in the way she addressed him that suggested a long acquaintance. David merely smiled, seemingly unperturbed by her gentle rebuke.

"You'll need to prepare for dinner service," he told Lucy and Peter. "There are uniforms in your room— nothing too formal, but we do maintain certain standards. I'll expect you back here at six-thirty to help with final preparations."

It was a dismissal, politely phrased but unmistakable. Lucy and Peter thanked Margaret for the tour and made their way back to their room, navigating the confusing corridors with slightly more confidence than before.

"What do you make of that?" Peter asked once they were alone in their room. "Margaret seems nice enough, but there's something..."

"Off," Lucy finished for him. "About all of this. The hotel, David, Margaret—it all feels like it's part of some play we've wandered into without knowing our lines."

Peter nodded in agreement, moving to the wardrobe where, as David had mentioned, two sets of uniforms hung waiting for them—black trousers and white shirts, simple but formal.

"We should get ready," he said after a moment. "Whatever's going on here, we need this job. At least for now."

Lucy knew he was right. Despite the strangeness of their situation, The Ornate Sapphire represented safety—a roof over their heads, regular meals, distance from the violence they had witnessed at The Trout Inn. They couldn't afford to let their suspicions drive them away, not when they had nowhere else to go.

They changed into the uniforms, which fit surprisingly well despite having been provided without any measurements being taken. Lucy felt a strange sense of transformation as she buttoned the crisp white shirt—as if she were stepping into a role, becoming someone else, someone whose past didn't include violence and hallucinations and desperate flights from the law.

"How do I look?" she asked Peter, attempting a smile.

"Like you belong here," he replied, his expression softening as he looked at her. "It suits you."

The simple compliment warmed her, pushing back some of the unease that had been building since their arrival. Whatever was happening at The Ornate Sapphire, at least they were facing it together.

At precisely six-thirty, they made their way back to the dining room, where David was waiting to brief them on their duties for the evening. The instructions were straightforward—serve the food that had been prepared by the unseen cook, keep wine glasses filled, clear plates between courses, and otherwise remain unobtrusive.

"Our residents value their privacy and their conversations," David explained. "They don't wish to be overheard or interrupted unnecessarily. Is that clear?"

They both nodded, though Lucy felt a twist of discomfort at the instruction. It seemed less about privacy and more about ensuring they didn't learn too much about the hotel's mysterious guests.

At seven o'clock, the residents began to arrive. Margaret Ellison came first, now dressed in an evening gown that seemed excessive for dinner at a remote hotel with only a handful of guests. She nodded politely to Lucy and Peter as she took her seat at the long table.

Next came a thin, nervous-looking man who introduced himself as Dr. Thomas Webb. He had a perpetual twitch in his left eye and kept glancing over his shoulder as if expecting someone to be following him. He took a seat across from Margaret, immediately reaching for the wine that Peter had poured.

The third arrival was a striking woman in her forties who entered with the confidence of someone accustomed to being watched. "Helena Blackwood," she said when Lucy pulled out her chair, her voice carrying a slight Eastern European accent. "You're the new girl, yes? How... refreshing."

There was something in the way Helena looked at her that made Lucy deeply uncomfortable an intensity that felt almost predatory. She was relieved when the woman's attention shifted to the entrance of the next guest.

The fourth resident was a man who must have been in his eighties, stooped and frail, leaning heavily on an ornately carved cane. He was introduced as Mr. Winters, though no first name was offered. Despite his apparent physical weakness, his eyes were sharp and alert, taking in every detail of Lucy's appearance with uncomfortable thoroughness.

The fifth and final resident to enter was the most unsettling of all. He was tall and broad-shouldered, perhaps in his fifties, with salt-and-pepper hair cut close to his scalp in a military style. He moved with a predator's grace, his eyes cold and assessing as they swept over Lucy and Peter.

"Colonel James Harrison," he introduced himself, his voice carrying a hint of an accent Lucy couldn't quite place. "You'll address me as 'Colonel,' not 'sir' or 'Mr. Harrison.' Is that understood?"

"Yes, Colonel," Lucy and Peter replied in unison, exchanging a quick glance that confirmed their shared discomfort.

David took his place at the head of the table, completing the group. "Now that we're all assembled," he announced, "shall we begin?"

What followed was one of the strangest dinners Lucy had ever experienced. The conversation around the table flowed with a peculiar rhythm, as if following rules only the residents understood. Topics would be introduced, briefly discussed, and then abandoned abruptly when they seemed on the verge of becoming interesting. Names were mentioned and then quickly retracted. References were made to events that were never fully explained.

Throughout it all, Lucy and Peter moved quietly around the table, serving food, pouring wine, clearing plates. They were treated as if they were invisible, the residents speaking freely despite their presence, yet never acknowledging them except to request more wine or another serving of food.

The meal itself was elaborate and expertly prepared—five courses of rich, flavourful dishes that seemed at odds with the remote location of the hotel. Lucy wondered about the mysterious cook David had mentioned, who apparently produced such sophisticated cuisine and then vanished without being seen.

As coffee was served at the end of the meal, the conversation around the table took a turn that caught Lucy's attention.

"Have you seen the news?" Dr. Webb asked, his voice slightly slurred from the wine he had consumed throughout dinner. "Another one gone missing. That makes five in the past two months."

"Thomas," Margaret chided gently, "we agreed not to discuss such unpleasant matters at dinner."

"But it's relevant," the doctor insisted, his nervous twitch more pronounced. "Especially with new staff. They should be warned—"

"That's quite enough," David interrupted sharply. "Lucy, Peter, you may clear the coffee service now and retire for the evening. Your duties are complete for today."

There was no room for argument in his tone. Lucy and Peter quickly cleared the remaining dishes and left the dining room, though Lucy couldn't help casting a final glance back at the table. Dr. Webb was being quietly but intensely reprimanded by David, while the other residents watched with varying expressions of concern and annoyance.

"What do you think he meant?" Lucy whispered to Peter as they made their way back to the kitchen with the loaded tray. "About people going missing?"

"I don't know," Peter replied, keeping his voice low. "But I don't like it. Any of it. The way they were talking, the way they looked at us... it's like they know something we don't."

Lucy nodded in agreement. The entire evening had left her with a growing sense of unease. There was something deeply wrong about The Ornate Sapphire and its residents—something beyond the usual eccentricities of the wealthy or privileged. These people weren't simply seeking privacy or escape; they were hiding something much darker.

After cleaning the kitchen as instructed, they made their way back to their room, both lost in their own thoughts about the strange dinner they had just served. The corridors seemed even more confusing in the dim evening light, shadows stretching and distorting in ways that played tricks on Lucy's perception.

As they turned a corner, Lucy glimpsed a figure at the far end of the hallway—a man standing perfectly still, watching them. The distance and poor lighting made it impossible to identify him, but something about his posture, the way he held himself, sent a chill of recognition through her.

"Peter," she whispered, grabbing his arm. "Look—"

But when Peter turned to look, the figure was gone, if it had ever been there at all. Lucy blinked, suddenly unsure of what she had seen. Was her mind playing tricks on her again? Was the medication failing?

"What is it?" Peter asked, concern evident in his voice.

"Nothing," Lucy said after a moment. "I thought I saw someone, but... it must have been a shadow."

Peter didn't look convinced, but he didn't press her further. They continued to their room in silence, each step feeling heavier than the last, as if the very air of The Ornate Sapphire was becoming thicker, more resistant to their passage.

Once safely behind the closed door of their room, Lucy sat on the edge of the bed, her hands trembling slightly. "Peter," she said quietly, "I don't think we should stay here. There's something wrong about this place, about these people."

Peter sighed, running a hand through his hair. "I know," he admitted. "But where else can we go? We have no money, no transportation. We're miles from anywhere."

The truth of his words settled heavily between them. They were trapped, at least for now, in this strange hotel with its mysterious residents and watchful corridors.

"One day at a time," Lucy reminded herself aloud. "We just need to keep our heads down, save whatever money we can, and figure out a plan."

Peter nodded, sitting beside her and taking her hand in his. The simple contact was reassuring, grounding her in reality when everything else seemed to be slipping into surreal territory.

"We'll be okay," he promised, though they both knew it was a promise he couldn't necessarily keep. "We've made it this far."

Lucy tried to take comfort in his words, in his presence beside her. But as she prepared for bed that night, taking her medication and changing into the nightclothes that had mysteriously appeared in the dresser drawer, she couldn't shake the feeling that they had walked willingly into a trap—one that had been set specifically for her.

Outside their window, the moon rose over the moors, casting silver light across the empty landscape. Somewhere in the distance, a lone figure stood watching the hotel, his face upturned to the particular window behind which Lucy now lay beside Peter, both of them drifting into uneasy sleep.

The watcher smiled in the darkness, knowing that everything was proceeding exactly as planned. Soon, very soon, Lucy Evans would come face to face with her deepest fears and her darkest impulses. And when that happened, he would be there to witness her final undoing.

Chapter 30:
Fractures

The first week at The Ornate Sapphire passed in a blur of routine. Lucy and Peter quickly settled into their roles, cleaning the public areas during the day, serving meals in the evening, and retreating to their room at night. The work wasn't difficult, though the layout of the hotel remained confusing, and Lucy occasionally found herself in corridors she didn't recognize, unsure of how she had gotten there.

The residents kept largely to themselves. Margaret Ellison would sometimes stop to chat when she encountered Lucy cleaning the lounge, offering snippets of the hotel's history or commenting on the weather, but never revealing anything personal. Dr. Webb hurried past with his nervous energy whenever they crossed paths, barely making eye contact. Helena Blackwood watched Lucy with that same unsettling intensity whenever she served at dinner, but spoke to her only to request more wine or another serving. Mr. Winters and Colonel Harrison remained distant and formal, treating the staff as if they were furniture rather than people.

David Mercer was an enigma, appearing and disappearing throughout the hotel with no discernible pattern. Sometimes he would stand in doorways or at the end of corridors, observing Lucy as she worked, his expression unreadable. Other times, he would be nowhere to be found for days, though his presence still seemed to permeate the building, as if he were somehow watching even when not physically present.

The mysterious cook remained unseen. Meals would appear in the kitchen, perfectly prepared and covered, ready to be served, yet neither Lucy nor Peter ever encountered the person who made them. When Lucy asked Margaret about this, the older woman merely smiled enigmatically and said, "The Ornate Sapphire has many secrets, my dear. It's best not to question them all at once."

On the eighth day, Lucy woke with a pounding headache. The morning light streaming through the window seemed too bright, too harsh, making her wince as she sat up in bed. Peter was already awake, buttoning his uniform shirt as he prepared for the day.

"You okay?" he asked, noticing her discomfort.

"Just a headache," she assured him, reaching for the bottle of medication on the nightstand. She frowned as she shook the bottle—it felt lighter than it should have. Opening it confirmed her suspicion: there were fewer pills than she expected, though she couldn't be certain how many should be left.

"Something wrong?" Peter asked, watching her expression.

"I don't think so," she said, though doubt crept into her voice. "I'm just not sure how many pills I've taken. I thought I had more left."

"Maybe you took an extra one without realizing?" Peter suggested. "You've been pretty tired some evenings."

That was true enough. The long days of work often left her exhausted, falling into bed and into sleep almost immediately. Perhaps she had taken her medication and simply forgotten about it.

"Probably," she agreed, swallowing a pill with a sip of water. "We should see if we can get to a pharmacy soon, though. I'll need a refill before too long."

Peter nodded, his expression betraying a hint of concern. They both knew how important Lucy's medication was for maintaining her stability, especially in this strange environment that seemed designed to unsettle them.

The headache persisted throughout the morning as Lucy went about her duties. The corridors seemed longer than usual, the shadows deeper, the silence more oppressive. As she dusted the ornate frames of paintings in the east wing, she found herself pausing frequently, certain she had heard footsteps behind her, only to turn and find the hallway empty.

By midday, she had developed a persistent sense that someone was watching her—not unusual in itself, given David's habit of observing the staff, but this felt different, more intimate somehow, as if the observer could see not just her physical form but her thoughts as well.

"You're getting paranoid," she muttered to herself, wringing out a cloth in a bucket of soapy water. "It's just the headache making you jumpy."

'Is it, though?' a familiar voice whispered in her ear.

Lucy froze, her heart skipping a beat. That voice—she hadn't heard it since arriving at The Ornate Sapphire, had begun to hope that perhaps the combination of medication and distance from her past had silenced it permanently.

"You're not real," she said firmly, though there was no one else in the corridor to hear her. "You're not here."

"Oh, but I am," Jim replied, his voice as clear as if he were standing right beside her. "I've always been here, Lucy. I'm part of you. You can't leave me behind."

Lucy squeezed her eyes shut, willing the voice to disappear. This couldn't be happening, not now, not when she had finally found some semblance of stability. She had been taking her medication regularly—hadn't she?

The doubt crept in, insidious and persistent. What if Peter was right? What if she had missed doses without realizing it? Or what if someone had been tampering with her pills? The thought seemed ridiculous, paranoid, yet she couldn't quite dismiss it.

'They're watching you,' Jim whispered, his voice taking on that conspiratorial tone she remembered all too well. 'They've been watching you from the beginning. Why do you think David brought you here?'

"Shut up," Lucy hissed, pressing her hands against her ears though she knew it would do nothing to silence a voice that came from within. "Just shut up."

'He knows, Lucy. He knows what you did to the homeless man. He knows about the brick, the blood, and the way you ran away afterward. And he's not the only one. They all know.'

A cold sweat broke out across Lucy's skin. It wasn't possible. No one could know about that night except Peter, and he had promised never to tell anyone. Yet doubt gnawed at her—the residents' strange behaviour, their cryptic conversations, the way they sometimes looked at her as if they were waiting for something to happen...

"Lucy?"

She gasped, spinning around to find Peter standing a few feet away, concern etched across his features.

"Are you okay?" he asked, taking a step closer. "You were talking to yourself."

"I'm fine," she lied, forcing a smile. "Just thinking out loud. This place gets too quiet sometimes."

Peter didn't look convinced, but he didn't press the issue. "David wants us to prepare the conservatory for some kind of gathering tonight," he said instead. "All the residents will be there, plus some guests arriving from out of town."

"Guests?" Lucy echoed, surprised. They hadn't had any new arrivals since they'd started working at the hotel.

"That's what he said." Peter shrugged. "Some kind of special occasion, apparently. We need to set up chairs, make sure the place is spotless. He was pretty insistent about it."

Lucy nodded, grateful for the distraction from her troubling thoughts. "Let's do it together," she suggested, already gathering her cleaning supplies. "I'm nearly done here anyway."

The conservatory was located at the rear of the hotel, a magnificent glass structure that extended from the main building like a crystal growth. Despite its grandeur, it had a neglected feel, as if it hadn't been used in some time. Dust covered the wrought iron furniture, and dead leaves had collected in the corners and beneath the large potted plants that dominated the space.

"Quite a job," Peter commented as they surveyed the room. "Why would they want to have a gathering in here when it's in such a state?"

Lucy didn't have an answer, but something about the space made her uneasy. The glass walls and ceiling created a fishbowl effect, making her feel exposed, observed from all angles. As the afternoon sun streamed through the panels, casting prismatic reflections across the floor, she had the distinct sensation of being caught in a web, with unseen predators circling just beyond the glass.

They worked in silence for a while, cleaning and arranging chairs in a semicircle facing a small raised platform at one end of the conservatory. The physical labour helped distract Lucy from her earlier episode, though she remained hyperaware of every sound, every shift in the light, and every movement in her peripheral vision.

"I wonder what kind of gathering this is," she said eventually, needing to break the silence. "It looks almost like they're setting up for a performance of some kind."

"Or a lecture," Peter suggested, adjusting the angle of a chair. "Maybe Dr. Webb is going to share his expertise on... whatever it is he's an expert in."

Lucy managed a small laugh at that. "Nervous twitching, perhaps? He's certainly mastered that."

Peter smiled, though his eyes retained that hint of concern as he looked at her. "You'd tell me if something was wrong, wouldn't you?" he asked suddenly. "If you were... hearing things again?"

The question caught her off guard. Had he noticed something? Was her distress more obvious than she'd thought?

"Of course," she assured him, though the lie felt heavy on her tongue. "I'm just tired. And this place... it gets to you after a while, doesn't it? All these corridors and shadows and strange people."

"Yeah," Peter agreed, his expression softening with relief. "It does. But we're okay. We've got each other."

The simple statement warmed her, pushing back some of the darkness that had been gathering at the edges of her mind. Peter had become her anchor in the storm, the one constant in a world that increasingly seemed to shift and distort around her.

They finished preparing the conservatory by late afternoon, leaving the space gleaming and ready for the evening's mysterious event. As they gathered their cleaning supplies to leave, David appeared in the doorway, seemingly materializing out of nowhere.

"Excellent work," he commented, surveying the room with an approving nod. "Everything is in perfect order."

"What's happening tonight?" Lucy asked before she could stop herself. "Some kind of performance?"

David's eyes fixed on her with that penetrating gaze that always made her feel as if he could see straight through her. "In a manner of speaking," he replied after a moment. "We have a tradition at The Ornate Sapphire—a gathering on certain significant dates where we share... stories. Experiences that have shaped us."

"Like a support group?" Peter asked, his tone carefully neutral.

A thin smile crossed David's face. "Something like that. Though our residents' stories tend to be more... unusual than most." He turned his attention back to Lucy. "You'll both be serving refreshments during the gathering. Simple drinks, nothing elaborate. Be in the kitchen at eight o'clock to prepare."

With that, he left, moving silently despite the hardwood floors that creaked beneath everyone else's footsteps.

"A storytelling circle," Peter murmured once David was gone. "Somehow I doubt they'll be sharing heartwarming childhood memories."

Lucy shivered despite the warmth of the conservatory. "No," she agreed. "I don't think 'heartwarming' is part of The Ornate Sapphire's vocabulary."

They returned to their room to rest before the evening's duties. Lucy's headache had subsided somewhat, but a new discomfort had taken its place—a strange sensation of disconnection, as if parts of her mind were floating free from her body, observing her actions from a distance.

She sat on the edge of the bed, studying her reflection in the mirror opposite. Her hair dye had begun to fade, the roots showing through in places, making her look somehow fragmented, divided between who she had been and who she was trying to become.

'You can't become someone else,' Jim's voice whispered, though his reflection didn't appear beside hers in the mirror. 'You can only ever be who you are. And we both know who that is, don't we, Lucy?'

She closed her eyes, willing the voice away, focusing on her breathing as she'd learned to do when the hallucinations became too persistent. In, out. In, out. Slow and steady, anchoring herself in the physical reality of her body.

When she opened her eyes again, she noticed something on the dresser that hadn't been there before—a small, ornate key made of tarnished bronze. She was certain it hadn't been there when they'd left for work that morning, yet here it was, its presence inexplicable and somehow threatening.

Lucy picked it up, feeling its weight in her palm. It was old, the design intricate and antique. What did it unlock? And more importantly, who had placed it in their room?

"Peter," she called, her voice slightly unsteady. "Did you put this here?"

Peter emerged from the bathroom, his hair damp from a shower. "Put what where?"

She held up the key. "This. I found it on the dresser, but it wasn't there this morning."

Peter frowned, taking the key from her and examining it. "Never seen it before," he confirmed. "Someone must have left it while we were working."

The implication hung in the air between them—someone had been in their room, touching their belongings, leaving mysterious objects for them to find. The violation of privacy sent a chill through Lucy.

"We should ask David about it," Peter suggested, though he didn't sound eager to do so. "It might be important."

"Or it might be some kind of test," Lucy said, the words emerging before she'd fully formed the thought. "To see how we react."

Peter looked at her sharply. "What do you mean?"

"I don't know," she admitted. "It's just a feeling. Like we're being... evaluated somehow. Like this whole place is some kind of experiment, and we're the subjects."

It sounded paranoid when spoken aloud, yet the expression on Peter's face suggested he'd had similar thoughts. The Ornate Sapphire had that effect—making the irrational seem plausible, the paranoid seem prudent.

"Let's just keep it to ourselves for now," Peter decided, pocketing the key. "See if anyone mentions it. If not... well, we'll figure it out."

Lucy nodded, though unease continued to gnaw at her. The key felt like a message, but she couldn't decipher its meaning. Was it an invitation? A warning? A trap?

As eight o'clock approached, they made their way to the kitchen to prepare for the gathering. As usual, there was no sign of the mysterious cook, but trays of canapés and pitchers of water and wine had been laid out, ready for them to serve.

They carried the refreshments to the conservatory, which had been transformed by the evening light. Candles had been placed throughout the space, casting flickering shadows across the glass walls. The chairs they had arranged earlier were now occupied by the residents, plus three people Lucy had never seen before—two men and a woman, all dressed in formal attire that seemed excessive for a simple gathering.

David stood on the small platform, addressing the group in low tones that fell silent as Lucy and Peter entered with the refreshment trays. All eyes turned to them, and Lucy felt that familiar sensation of being examined, assessed, and judged.

"Ah, perfect timing," David said smoothly. "Our evening's entertainment is about to begin."

Lucy and Peter moved around the semicircle, offering drinks and canapés to the assembled guests. When Lucy reached Helena Blackwood, the woman caught her wrist in a grip that was surprisingly strong.

"You feel it, don't you?" Helena murmured, her eyes locked on Lucy's face. "The thinning of the veil. The blurring of boundaries. It's already beginning."

Before Lucy could respond, Helena released her and took a glass of wine, turning her attention back to David as if nothing had happened. Lucy continued serving, her wrist still tingling where Helena had gripped it, the woman's strange words echoing in her mind.

Once everyone had been served, David motioned for Lucy and Peter to stand at the back of the room, ready to refill glasses as needed. The gathering was about to begin in earnest.

"Friends, residents, honoured guests," David began, his voice carrying easily through the conservatory. "We gather, as is our tradition, to share the stories that have brought us to this place of sanctuary. To speak of the unspeakable, to acknowledge the darkness that lives within us all."

A murmur of appreciation ran through the assembled group, as if David had said something profound rather than vague and slightly menacing.

"Tonight," he continued, "we have a special focus for our gathering. A theme, if you will." His eyes found Lucy's across the room, locking onto her with uncomfortable intensity. "Tonight, we speak of delusion. Of the mind's capacity to create its own reality, and of what happens when that reality collides with the world outside."

Lucy's heart began to race, her palms growing damp with sweat. This couldn't be a coincidence. The topic was too specific, too relevant to her own struggles. It felt deliberately chosen, a targeted probe into her deepest vulnerabilities.

'See?' Jim whispered in her ear. 'I told you they know. They've always known. This whole thing is about you, Lucy. It always has been.'

She gripped the serving tray tighter, using the pressure against her fingers as an anchor to reality. This was just paranoia, she told herself. Just her illness manifesting again because she was tired and stressed and possibly missing doses of her medication.

Yet as the gathering continued, Lucy found it increasingly difficult to maintain that rational perspective. One by one, the residents stood to share their stories—tales of mental breakdowns, of psychotic episodes, of violence committed in the grip of delusion. Each narrative seemed to echo aspects of her own experiences, as if they were pulling fragments of her life from her mind and weaving them into their stories.

Dr. Webb spoke of a patient who bludgeoned a stranger to death in the grip of paranoid psychosis, convinced the man was a demon sent to drag him to hell. Margaret Ellison recounted witnessing a young woman's descent into schizophrenia, culminating in an attack on a loved one who had only been trying to help. Helena Blackwood described the sensation of losing touch with reality, of being unable to distinguish between what was real and what was imagined.

With each story, Lucy felt herself slipping further away from the present moment, as if the narrative was pulling her back into her own past, forcing her to relive her most traumatic experiences. The conservatory seemed to shift around her, the glass walls closing in, the candlelight creating shadows that moved independently of their sources.

'It's happening again,' Jim's voice observed with what sounded like satisfaction. 'You're losing your grip, Lucy. Just like before. Just like always.'

"No," she whispered, too quietly for anyone to hear. "I'm fine. This is real. I'm here."

But where was "here," exactly? The conservatory had begun to blend with other places in her memory—the alleyway where she'd attacked the homeless man, her bedroom where she thought she'd stabbed Jim, the street outside the B&B where she'd nearly been hit by a car. Reality was becoming fluid, malleable, and unreliable.

She became aware that Peter was watching her with concern that her breathing had become rapid and shallow, that her hands were trembling visibly. She needed air, space, distance from these stories that seemed designed to trigger her worst impulses.

"Excuse me," she murmured to Peter. "Bathroom. I'll be right back."

Before he could respond, she slipped out of the conservatory, moving quickly through the darkened corridors of the hotel. She had no particular destination in mind, only the desperate need to escape the suffocating atmosphere of the gathering.

She found herself in a part of the hotel she didn't recognize—a narrow corridor with peeling wallpaper and flickering lights. The floor creaked beneath her feet, the sound unnaturally loud in the silence. As she moved forward, she realized with growing unease that the corridor seemed to be lengthening ahead of her, stretching impossibly far into the distance.

'You can't escape,' Jim's voice informed her, now sounding as if it came from somewhere in front of her rather than inside her head. 'You can't run from who you are, Lucy. You can't run from what you've done.'

"Leave me alone," she pleaded, her voice cracking with emotion. "Just leave me alone."

'But you need me,' Jim insisted. 'Without me, who would remind you of the truth? Who would keep you honest? Peter? He doesn't even know who you really are. If he did, he'd run screaming in the other direction.'

"That's not true," Lucy said, more forcefully this time. "Peter knows me. The real me."

'Does he?' Jim's voice was mocking now. 'Does he know about the others? The ones before the homeless man? The ones you've tried so hard to forget?'

Lucy stopped walking, her blood turning to ice in her veins. "There weren't any others," she whispered. "You're lying."

Jim responded, 'Am I? Or are you the one lying to yourself, Lucy? Hiding behind your medication, your makeover, your new identity. But you can't change what you are. You can only hide it for a while.'

She pressed her hands against her ears, backing up against the wall, trying to shut out the voice that seemed to be coming from everywhere at once now. "Stop it," she gasped. "Just stop."

"Lucy?"

The sound of Peter's voice cut through her panic like a knife through fog. She opened her eyes to find him standing a few feet away, his face creased with worry. The impossible corridor had vanished; they were in a normal hallway not far from the conservatory.

"Are you okay?" he asked, taking a step toward her. "You've been gone for a while. I was worried."

Lucy stared at him, trying to reconcile the sudden shift in her perception. Lucy's eyes' bloodshot, her eyes twitching rapidly, trying to decipher her environment.

"I'm fine," she said automatically, the lie coming easily to her lips. "Just needed some air. Those stories were... intense."

Peter's expression suggested he didn't believe her, but before he could press further, David appeared behind him, his tall figure silhouetted against the dim light of the corridor.

"Is everything alright?" he inquired, his tone solicitous though his eyes remained cold and assessing. "You seemed... affected by our gathering."

Lucy straightened, pulling herself together with an effort of will. "I'm fine," she repeated. "Just tired. It's been a long day."

"Indeed it has," David agreed smoothly. "Perhaps you should retire for the night. Peter can handle the rest of the service. The gathering is nearly concluded anyway."

It was a dismissal couched as consideration, and Lucy lacked the energy to argue. She nodded, grateful for the excuse to escape.

"Thank you," she said, already turning toward the staircase that would lead her back to their room. "Good night."

As she climbed the stairs, she could feel both men watching her—Peter with concern, David with something more calculating. The sensation of being observed, evaluated, judged, followed her all the way to her room, where she closed and locked the door behind her with a sense of profound relief.

The room was dark, the only light coming from the moon outside the window. Lucy didn't turn on the lamp, preferring the concealing shadows as she sank onto the bed, her body trembling with the aftermath of her episode.

She was slipping again. Despite the medication, despite all her efforts to maintain control. Jim's voice, the distortions in her perception, the paranoid thoughts about being watched and tested—all signs that her mind was fracturing once more.

'It never really stopped,' Jim's voice observed from the darkest corner of the room. 'You just got better at ignoring it for a while. But I was always here, Lucy. Always waiting.'

Lucy turned toward the voice, and for the first time since arriving at The Ornate Sapphire, she saw him—not just heard his voice, but saw his form materializing from the shadows. Jim stood by the window, his familiar smirk in place, and his eyes reflecting the moonlight with an unnatural gleam.

"You're not real," she said, more to herself than to the apparition. "You're in my head. A manifestation of my illness."

'Maybe,' Jim conceded, moving closer to the bed. 'Or maybe I'm something more. A messenger. A warning. A reminder of what happens when you try to bury the truth.'

As he spoke, his form seemed to shift, becoming at once more solid and more amorphous, as if he existed in multiple states simultaneously. Lucy found she couldn't look away, mesmerized by the impossible physics of his presence.

'They're coming for you, Lucy,' he whispered, leaning down until his face was inches from hers. 'All of them. They know what you did, what you're capable of. And they won't stop until they've exposed you, broken you, destroyed you completely.'

"Who?" Lucy demanded, her voice stronger than she expected. "Who's coming for me?"

Jim's smile widened, revealing teeth that seemed too sharp, too numerous. 'Everyone. David. The residents. Even Peter.'

"Peter would never hurt me," Lucy insisted, though a seed of doubt had been planted. "He's the only one I can trust."

'Is he?' Jim questioned, his form beginning to dissolve at the edges, melting back into the shadows. 'Then why did he lie about the key?'

Before Lucy could ask what he meant, Jim had vanished completely, leaving her alone in the darkened room with only his lingering words for company. What key? The bronze one they had found on the dresser? How had Peter lied about it?

She was still turning these questions over in her mind when the door opened and Peter entered, looking tired but relieved to find her safely in their room.

"The gathering's over," he reported, loosening his tie. "Everyone's gone back to their rooms. It was... strange. The whole night was strange."

Lucy watched him move around the room, preparing for bed with his usual methodical habits. Could Jim be right? Could Peter be part of whatever was happening at The Ornate Sapphire? The thought seemed absurd, paranoid, yet she couldn't quite dismiss it.

"Peter," she said suddenly, "where's the key? The one we found earlier?"

He paused in the act of removing his shirt, a slight tension entering his shoulders. "What key?"

The response sent a chill through her. "The bronze one. The antique. You put it in your pocket before we went down for the gathering."

Peter turned to face her, his expression unreadable in the dim light. "Lucy," he said carefully, "we didn't find any key. I don't know what you're talking about."

The room seemed to tilt around her, reality shifting once again. Had she imagined the key? But no, she remembered it clearly—the weight of it in her palm, the intricate design, the tarnished metal. It had been real. It had to have been.

"You're lying," she whispered, backing away from him. "Why are you lying to me?"

Peter's expression shifted from confusion to concern. "I'm not lying, Lucy. There was no key. I think... I think you might be having some problems with your medication again. Are you hearing things? Seeing things?"

Lucy's back hit the wall; there was nowhere left to retreat. "Stop it," she said, her voice rising. "Stop pretending like I'm crazy. I know what I saw. I know what we found."

Peter approached slowly, hands held up in a placating gesture. "Lucy, please. You're not well. Let me help you. We can figure this out together."

But all Lucy could hear was Jim's warning echoing in her mind: 'They're coming for you. All of them. Even Peter.'

As Peter reached for her, his expression full of concern that now seemed false, manipulative, Lucy made a decision. She couldn't trust anyone at The Ornate Sapphire—not David, not the residents, and most devastatingly, not even Peter. She was alone in her struggle, alone with the truth that everyone else seemed determined to deny.

Chapter 31:
The Unravelling

Sleep eluded Lucy that night. She lay rigidly on her side of the bed, keeping as much distance from Peter as possible, listening to his breathing as it eventually deepened into the rhythm of sleep. The moonlight crept across the floor with agonizing slowness, marking the passage of hours that felt like centuries.

Her mind raced with questions, possibilities, fears. What if everything—the entire experience at The Ornate Sapphire—had been orchestrated specifically to trigger her breakdown? The residents with their disturbing stories, David with his penetrating gaze and cryptic comments, even Peter with his inexplicable lies about the key... all of it could be part of an elaborate scheme to push her over the edge.

'But why me?' she thought, despair creeping in. 'What do they want?'

Jim's voice, now a constant companion, a twisted confidant, whispered in her mind: 'They don't want anything personal. It's not about you, Lucy. It's about what you represent. A case study. An opportunity.'

She tossed and turned, unable to find a comfortable position, the weight of her racing thoughts crushing her. The air in the room seemed to thicken, pressing down on her, making it hard to breathe.

'What do they want me to do?' she wondered, her heart pounding in her chest. 'What's the end game here?'

As if in answer, fragments of conversations she'd overheard, snippets of the residents' stories, and David's carefully chosen words flashed through her mind, coalescing into a chilling realization. They weren't just trying to break her; they were trying to control her. To understand the precise levers that could turn a person like her—someone with a history of mental illness and violence—into a weapon.

'They're not interested in healing me, they're studying me, she thought with growing horror. They want to know how to make more like me. How to weaponize madness.' But why? What possible reason could anyone have for targeting her this way?

'You know why,' Jim's voice whispered from the shadows. 'They want to see you break. They want to witness your madness, your violence. It excites them.'

A short time later, after Peter had woken up and left the room, Lucy noticed something in the bedside table drawer that hadn't been there before—a small bronze key, identical to the one she had found in their room the previous day. The key Peter had claimed didn't exist. Lucy stared at it, her heart pounding in her chest. Was this another hallucination? Or was it proof that she hadn't imagined the first key that Peter had lied to her for reasons she couldn't begin to comprehend? With trembling fingers, she picked up the key. It felt solid, real, the metal cool against her skin. She turned it over in her palm, examining the intricate design. It was definitely the same key—or at least, identical to the one she remembered finding.

Lucy began to question the very nature of her reality at The Ornate Sapphire. The medication, the carefully crafted environment, the constant manipulation of her senses—it all seemed designed to blur the lines between what was real and what was not. If she couldn't trust her own mind, how could she be sure that anything at The Ornate Sapphire was as it seemed?" They're not just trying to break you," Jim whispered, his voice laced with something akin to admiration. "They're trying to rewrite you. To erase your past and replace it with a reality of their own making." It was a terrifying thought, but it also gave her a strange sense of power. If her perception was so easily manipulated, then perhaps she could learn to manipulate it herself.

There was a small keyhole in the painting above the bed gone completely unnoticed until now, almost invisible unless you were looking directly at it. Lucy glanced over her shoulder, confirming she was on her own, before reaching into her pocket for the bronze key. It fit perfectly into the keyhole. Lucy hesitated only briefly before turning it, hearing a soft click as some mechanism within the frame released. The painting swung outward like a door, revealing a small recess in the wall. Inside was a leather-bound notebook, old and worn, its pages yellowed with age. Heart pounding, Lucy removed the notebook and quickly closed the painting-door, pocketing the key once more. She slipped the notebook into the pocket of her uniform jacket, which was fortunately large enough to conceal its presence. The cover bore no title or name, just a strange symbol embossed in faded gold—a triangle with an eye at its centre, surrounded by intricate patterns that seemed to shift and change if she looked at them too long. Lucy opened it carefully, aware that the aged pages might be fragile. A cold feeling settled in Lucy's stomach as she read. The notebook detailed experiments conducted on a series of "subjects," focusing on methods to induce hallucinations, paranoia, and eventually violence. The clinical tone, the methodical documentation of suffering, made it all the more horrifying.

Lucy struggled to reconcile the Ornate Sapphire's remote location and outdated facade with the sophisticated experiment it housed. It seemed impossible that such a clandestine operation could thrive without attracting attention. But then, she considered the wealth and influence David clearly wielded. Perhaps the Ornate Sapphire was just one piece of a much larger network, funded by shadowy organizations and shielded by powerful individuals who benefited from its research.

'Don't underestimate the power of money and secrecy,' Jim whispered, as if reading her thoughts. 'Some things are better left unseen, and those who have the means will ensure they remain that way.' Perhaps the Ornate Sapphire was just one piece of a much larger network, funded by shadowy organizations and shielded by powerful individuals who benefited from its research. The idea only served to further unsettle her.

The discovery of the notebook had opened Lucy's eyes to the true nature of The Ornate Sapphire. It wasn't just a place for treating mental illness; it was a laboratory for manipulating and controlling the human mind.

As she delved deeper into the notebook, she uncovered details of previous experiments that sent chills down her spine. One section described a replication of Zimbardo's prison experiment, where patients were assigned roles as "guards" and "prisoners" and subjected to increasingly abusive treatment.

The "guards," fuelled by a sense of authority and anonymity, quickly descended into sadism, subjecting the "prisoners" to psychological torture, humiliation, and even physical abuse. Unlike the original experiment which had to be shut down prematurely due to the extreme distress and trauma experienced by the participants, the power dynamic was analysed further with blunt objects mysteriously appearing in the prison setting. With the guards encouraged to further degrade the prisoners in this experiment, this culminated in a prison riot where the majority of participants died.

Lucy shuddered, imagining the horrors that had unfolded within the walls of The Ornate Sapphire. It wasn't just about treating mental illness; it was about exploiting it, pushing people to their breaking points, and seeing what they were capable of.

Another section of the notebook described a replication of Dr. Stanley Milgram's obedience to authority experiment. Patients were instructed to administer actual electric shocks to a "learner" for every wrong answer they gave on a test.

The "teachers," despite their moral reservations, continued to administer increasingly powerful shocks, egged on by the authority figure in the lab coat. Some of them even witnessed the "learner" convulsing and screaming in pain, but they still obeyed the instructions, driven by a deep-seated desire to please authority and avoid punishment.

Lucy felt a wave of nausea wash over her, realizing the extent of the manipulation and control that was being exerted at The Ornate Sapphire. It wasn't just about studying human behaviour; it was about exploiting people's vulnerabilities and pushing them to commit acts they would never have thought possible.

As she continued to read, she realized that The Ornate Sapphire wasn't just about observing human behaviour; it was about actively shaping it, moulding it, and breaking it down until it conformed to their twisted ideals.

She thought of the news reports she'd seen on TV in London—the riots, the xenophobic attacks, the growing unrest. What if this was all connected? What if Project Threshold wasn't just about understanding psychosis, but about harnessing it, weaponizing it for some twisted political agenda?

She had to get out. She had to warn someone, somehow. But who would believe her? She was, after all, a schizophrenic with a history of violence. Who would take her seriously?

'You can't trust anyone, Lucy,' Jim whispered, his voice a constant, insidious presence. 'They're all part of it. Even Peter.'

The thought sent a jolt of panic through her. Peter had seemed so genuine, so caring. But what if it was all an act? What if he was simply playing a role, manipulating her emotions to further the experiment?

She looked at him sleeping peacefully beside her, his face relaxed and unguarded. Was this the face of a co-conspirator? Of a manipulator? Or was it the face of someone who genuinely cared for her, someone who was now in grave danger because of his association with her?

'You have to know,' Jim urged. 'You have to be sure.'

Driven by a desperate need for clarity, Lucy slipped out of bed, moving as quietly as possible so as not to wake Peter. She crept to the dresser where she kept her medication, her heart pounding in her chest.

She needed to know, once and for all, if the pills were being tampered with. If they were, it would confirm her worst fears—that she was a pawn in a game far bigger than herself.

With trembling fingers, she opened the bottle and examined the remaining pills, comparing them to the images she had found online. They looked the same—small, white, and round. But were they? Or had they been replaced with something else, something designed to push her over the edge?

She needed to test them, to analyse their chemical composition. But how? She had no scientific equipment, no access to a laboratory. All she had was her own intuition, her own desperate need to know the truth.

An idea formed in her mind, reckless and dangerous but perhaps her only option. She would take one of the pills, but not swallow it. Instead, she would hold it under her tongue, allowing it to dissolve slowly, paying close attention to the sensations it produced. If it was the real medication, she knew what to expect—a gradual calming of her racing thoughts, a lessening of the voices, a sense of groundedness. But if it was something else... something designed to amplify her psychosis... she would know it immediately.

It was a risk, a dangerous gamble with her own sanity. But she couldn't see any other way to be sure. She had to know the truth, even if it destroyed her.

With a trembling hand, she placed a pill under her tongue, closing her eyes and waiting for the effects to begin.

At first, nothing happened. She felt only the familiar taste of the tablet dissolving slowly in her mouth, a slight bitterness that she had grown accustomed to over the years. Minutes ticked by, each one feeling like an eternity. The silence in the room was broken only by Peter's steady breathing and the frantic pounding of her own heart.

Then, gradually, subtly, she began to notice a change. A slight tingling sensation at the base of her skull, a faint pressure behind her eyes. The shadows in the room seemed to deepen, to take on a more menacing quality. The voices in her head, which had been relatively quiet since arriving at The Ornate Sapphire, began to stir, whispering and murmuring just below the threshold of her awareness.

'It's working,' Jim's voice observed with a hint of excitement. 'They're turning up the heat.'

Lucy swallowed hard, trying to ignore the rising tide of anxiety. She focused on her breathing, on the physical sensations in her body, desperately trying to anchor herself in the present moment. But it was becoming increasingly difficult. The hallucinations were growing stronger, more vivid. The shadows were no longer just shadows; they were taking on shapes, faces, grotesque forms that seemed to leer at her from the corners of the room.

She felt a sudden urge to move, to run, to escape the suffocating confines of the room. The Ornate Sapphire was no longer a sanctuary but a trap, a cage designed to hold her captive while her mind unravelled.

She had to get out. She had to find Peter. She had to warn him about what was happening, before it was too late.

Driven by a desperate need to act, Lucy pulled away from the wall, her legs unsteady beneath her. She stumbled toward the door, her hand reaching for the handle, her mind racing with a frantic urgency that threatened to overwhelm her completely.

The handle turned under her touch; it wasn't Peter she was staring at. It was David.

He was stood right in front of the door, his face calm.

"I suggest you don't do that", he said.

"Where's Peter!", Lucy screamed.

David smiled, 'Don't worry about Peter. He's in a safe space. You have a big night ahead of you, you need your rest'.

He moved to leave and locked the door behind him.

As David's footsteps faded away, Lucy began to panic. She grabbed the door and tried to open it, but it was locked. She was trapped.

"What's happening?", she screamed.

Jim responded, 'It's begun, Lucy. It's what you have always wanted. You are going to be completely free!'.

Lucy stumbled back, the madness beginning to take hold. Lucy was trapped, with no way out. The weight of the situation crashed down on her, as she sunk to the floor crying.

Lucy pulled the notebook from her pocket, opening it again to confirm she hadn't imagined its contents. The clinical descriptions of induced psychosis, the photograph of her, the final entry about "Subject 28"—it was all real, tangible evidence of the nightmare she had stumbled into.

As she flipped through the pages once more, a detail caught her eye that she had missed in her initial shock—a reference to medication being "adjusted" to accelerate the subjects' deterioration. The realization hit her like a physical blow: her pills. The ones that had been mysteriously disappearing from the bottle. They must have been tampering with her medication, either reducing the dosage or replacing it entirely with something designed to trigger her psychosis rather than suppress it.

CHAPTER 32:
INTO THE ABYSS

Jim was sat on the edge of Lucy's bed. She could see Jim now all the time. She was in her room. 'They are waiting for you Lucy, you need to do what they want' Jim said. 'I can't, it's not right' Lucy responded. 'You can't help it, it's who you are, but don't worry Lucy, I will be there with you', Jim replied. Jim vanished and was replaced by Peter. 'Lucy, what's happening are you okay' Peter asked.

'I don't know what to do' Lucy responded. She reached out to him, his face a picture of pain and regret, only it wasn't Peter. It was Jim, he was back. 'I'm sorry, Lucy,' he said, and as he drew closer, he whispered something in her ear, it echoed off the walls as she dropped to the floor.

It was then that she realized, there was no escaping. She was going to end it all; there was nothing else she could do.

That was the voice of Lucy, but that wasn't what Lucy was thinking. It was the thoughts of the experiment, the data, the numbers.

David walked into the room.

"Are you ready Lucy?" David asked.

Lucy didn't respond.

"It's time for you to play your part" David said.

Lucy stood up and walked towards David.

"You have done this to me; you have messed up my mind" Lucy responded.

David smirked.

"We just gave you the opportunity to show who you are," he said.

David began to lead Lucy away.

"Where are we going?" Lucy asked.

David didn't respond.

They arrived at a large door, Lucy noticed they were in the amphitheatre. She could see all the people looking at her. Peter was tied to a chair. They put earmuffs on Lucy whilst David addressed the crowd.

David began to speak, "Ladies and Gentlemen, we are here today to witness the end of Project Threshold. As you are aware, we have been following Lucy for many years now, and we have been watching her.

We have been manipulating her environment for some time now to test what effect this has on her perceptions of reality through a number of different means and it has all come to this." David continued; "after learning of the tragic demise of Lucy's mother, we wondered what effect trauma and a sense of abandonment from a young age would have on future relationships, behaviours and whether there is a direct link between trauma and psychosis. Once schizophrenic episodes started to occur, we wondered what effect social and environmental cues have on psychotic breakdowns. As a firm believer in environmental determinism, I believe free will is an illusion, I wanted to test this."

"Has the social world around her served as nothing more than a carefully orchestrated plot to trigger paranoia, not exactly. You see, we've discovered something fascinating, due to the faint line between reality and delusion, Lucy only hurts those close to her that try to help her. With the right stimuli, can we trigger her paranoia to do exactly that?"

"Phase One complete," David announced clinically. "The subject is demonstrating heightened paranoid response to environmental triggers. Note the elevated respiratory rate and pupil dilation."

Lucy's world began to spin. The faces in the amphitheatre blurred together, their clinical gazes burning into her. She could hear their pens scratching against notepads, documenting her every reaction like she was some lab specimen.

"What you're about to witness," David continued, "is the culmination of years of careful environmental manipulation. Every detail of Lucy's life - from the timing of her mother's death to her seemingly random encounters in London - was orchestrated to test our hypothesis: that human behaviour, particularly in those with predisposition to psychosis, can be precisely controlled through environmental stimuli alone."

The audience murmured with interest as David gestured to a large screen behind him. "Our network of businesses - the taxi service that brought her here, the disposal company that cleaned up after her episodes, our monitoring systems throughout London - all served to create a controlled environment without her knowledge. We didn't need to implant thoughts or manipulate her mind directly. We simply needed to understand the triggers that would lead her to act exactly as we predicted."

Lucy's vision blurred. The room seemed to pulse with each word David spoke. She could see Peter struggling against his restraints, trying to catch her eye, but his face kept morphing into Jim's and back again.

"The final phase," David announced, "will demonstrate how complete environmental control can override even the strongest emotional bonds. Subject 28 will eliminate the very person she believes she loves most - not because we tell her to, but because we've created a reality where she believes she has no other choice."

The lights dimmed. A series of images began flashing on the screens around them - fragments of Lucy's past, distorted and twisted. The homeless man's face. Her mother's body. Jim's blood on her hands. Each image triggered a cascade of memories, but Lucy could no longer tell which were real and which had been planted by these people.

"Please," she whispered, but she wasn't sure who she was begging - David, the audience, or the demons in her own mind.

Peter's voice cut through the chaos: "Lucy, look at me! This isn't real! None of this is real!"

But as she turned toward him, the room shifted again. Peter's face flickered between expressions of love and murderous rage. The knife appeared in her hand - had it been there all along? The audience leaned forward in their seats, pens poised.

"The subject will now demonstrate that given the right environmental conditions, even the strongest human connections become meaningless," David's voice echoed. "Free will is an illusion. We are all simply products of our environment."

The spotlight went out, plunging Lucy into total darkness for a heartbeat before a new, blood-red light illuminated the scene. The conservatory had vanished completely now, replaced by a featureless black chamber with a single object at its centre—a knife, its blade gleaming crimson in the unnatural light. 'Take it,' Jim urged, his mouth suddenly next to her ear. 'Take it and end this. It's the only way out.' With trembling hands, Lucy reached for the knife. The moment her fingers closed around the handle, a surge of violent energy coursed through her body, igniting every nerve ending with an almost pleasurable fire. The sensation was overwhelming, intoxicating, a release of every dark impulse she had ever suppressed.

Lucy turned, the knife clutched tightly in her hand, to find Peter standing before her— Lucy felt her arm rise, the knife gleaming. Peter's face kept changing - friend, enemy, saviour, threat. The room spun faster. The audience watched. David smiled.

Peter looked afraid but determined, his hands raised in a placating gesture. "Lucy," he said gently, "It's me. It's Peter. Put down the knife." From the darkness surrounding them, David's voice drifted in like smoke: "The catalyst is applied. Begin final observation sequence." Peter took a careful step toward her. "Whatever you're seeing, whatever they're making you see—it's not real. I'm real. We're real. Remember the B&B? Remember the early days, the fun we had? Remember how we promised to get through this together?"

His words penetrated the fog of delusion, creating a moment of clarity in Lucy's fractured consciousness. She saw Peter clearly now, saw the conservatory behind him, saw the audience watching with predatory anticipation.

"They want me to kill you," she whispered, the knife suddenly heavy in her hand. "That's what this whole thing has been leading to."

Peter nodded slowly. "I know. But you don't have to do what they want. You're stronger than they think."

For a moment, Lucy felt herself regaining control, fighting back against the drug, the stimuli, the careful manipulations designed to trigger her violent impulses. Peter was right—she didn't have to be what they wanted her to be. She could choose differently. She could break the cycle.

'But it's not that simple, is it?' Jim's voice cut through her momentary clarity. 'Because they're right about one thing, Lucy. This is who you are. Who you've always been.'

And with those words, the hallucinatory world shifted again. Peter's face blurred, transforming before her eyes into her father's face, twisted with the same cold indifference he had shown throughout her childhood. Then it changed again, becoming the homeless man she had attacked with the brick. Then Jim. Then back to Peter, but a Peter with cruel eyes and a mocking smile, a Peter who knew all her secrets and despised her for them.

'You're pathetic,' this not-Peter sneered. 'A broken little girl playing at being normal. Did you really think I could love someone like you? Someone so damaged, so violent, so beyond redemption?'

"Stop it," Lucy whispered, backing away. "You're not Peter. Peter would never say those things."

'Wouldn't I?' the apparition challenged. 'I've seen the real you, Lucy. The monster behind the mask. And now you'll see it too.'

He lunged toward her suddenly, hands outstretched as if to grab her. Lucy reacted instinctively, the knife in her hand moving in a swift arc through the air, connecting with solid flesh.

The hallucination shattered like glass, reality rushing back in a flood of horrifying clarity. Lucy stood in the centre of the conservatory, the knife buried in Peter's chest—the real Peter, blood blooming across his white shirt as he stared at her with an expression of shock and betrayal.

"Lucy?" he gasped, his voice barely audible as he crumpled to his knees. "Why?"

The knife slipped from Lucy's numb fingers, clattering to the floor as Peter collapsed completely, blood pooling beneath him on the polished tiles. The conservatory was silent, the audience watching with clinical detachment as Lucy fell to her knees beside Peter's body, her hands pressing futilely against the wound.

"No," she sobbed, the reality of what she had done crashing over her like a wave. "No, no, no. Peter, please. I didn't mean to. I thought—I saw—"

But Peter couldn't hear her anymore. His eyes stared upward, unseeing, the life already fading from them as blood continued to pump from the wound in his chest.

From the platform, David's voice cut through Lucy's grief like a knife: "Experiment complete. Subject 28 has fulfilled parameters as predicted. Data collection phase will commence in thirty minutes, once subject has processed the implications of her actions."

A small camera in the corner of the room whirred softly, recording every detail of Lucy's breakdown. David's eyes gleamed with satisfaction; he knew he had done the right thing. In his mind he was saving humanity, one tortured soul at a time.

Lucy barely registered his words, her entire being focused on Peter's lifeless form before her. She had done this. Despite all her awareness of the manipulation, despite her determination to resist, she had played right into their hands. She had become exactly what they wanted her to be—a killer, a subject, a success in their twisted experiment.

"I'm so sorry," she whispered, cradling Peter's head in her lap, her tears falling onto his still face. "I'm so sorry."

The residents and guests began to file out of the conservatory, their purpose fulfilled, their entertainment concluded. Lucy remained on the floor, holding Peter's body, lost in a grief so profound it threatened to consume her entirely.

Only Jim remained, standing over her with an expression of something almost like pity on his spectral face. 'What did I tell you, Lucy?' he said softly. 'This is who you are. This is who you've always been.'

And in that moment, Lucy knew he was right. No matter how hard she tried to change; to escape her nature, violence followed her like a shadow, destroying everything and everyone she touched. First the homeless man, now Peter—and who knew how many others she had forgotten or suppressed?

She was broken beyond repair, dangerous beyond redemption. And there was only one thing left to do.

Chapter 33:
The Final Station

Dawn bled quietly over a lonely platform on the edge of a forgotten station. 'Was this real?' Lucy wondered, trying to ground herself in the cold air, the rough texture of her coat. But the platform felt as dreamlike as her memories, as if she were caught between two worlds, belonging to neither. For hours—or was it days?—she had wandered from The Ornate Sapphire, a place of unspeakable experiments and relentless manipulation, leaving behind a maelstrom of pain and questions. London was a faded memory now, its concrete edges blurred by doubt; even the police were nowhere to be seen. Had they ever been involved at all, or was that just another layer in the labyrinth of her misbegotten reality?

She sat on a cold wooden bench, the silence around her broken only by the soft, irregular tick of an ancient clock mounted on a peeling wall. In that still moment, every echo in her mind stirred questions that left her trembling: How could an experiment like The Ornate Sapphire have been allowed to unfold in broad daylight? Why did no one come for the victim—or for herself—after the chaos that had been meticulously orchestrated? And most piercing of all, could any of it have really happened? Reality, after all, had been as malleable as the nightmares that pursued her every step.

A battered leather notebook slipped from her pocket as she shifted, fluttering open on the bench. It was filled with cryptic entries and fragmented evidence of experiments and unspeakable procedures. In a trembling whisper she wondered if this book might be her only chance to challenge their narrative—a clue for future investigators, or perhaps just another red herring in a game with no rules.

As the light deepened, the distant sound of a train's horn cut through the stillness. The train hurtled closer, its metallic roar gradually overwhelming the quiet desolation that had become Lucy's world. The platform was empty save for a scattering of wary onlookers, whose eyes slid off her as if she were a ghost meant to vanish. They did not come to offer comfort or ask what had become of her life—perhaps afraid to confront the ambiguity that shrouded her very existence. Or perhaps, like her, they simply suspected nothing was as it seemed.

Lucy's mind wandered to that critical moment within The Ornate Sapphire—echoes of manipulated memory, voices insisting she must accept the inevitable, the singular answer to a lifetime of betrayal and violence. Jim's voice, or what she thought was Jim's voice, echoed in her mind: 'You always have a choice, Lucy. But do you really? Or are you just a puppet dancing on their strings?' And yet the crushing allure of finality, of erasing every painful remembrance and unanswered question, beckoned irresistibly. Was it possible that ending it all might finally separate what was real from what had been fabricated?

Her gaze fell on a yellow line painted along the platform's edge. Time and again she had seen it as a boundary between safety and oblivion. The rumbling train now straddled the horizon, its engine growling a fatal invitation. Lucy stepped off the bench, drawn inexorably toward that ultimate threshold. Every footstep resounded with the weight of all her miseries and uncertainties—of every manipulated memory, every orchestrated tragedy, and every unanswered question that clung to her like a shroud.

In that suspended moment, doubt churned in her heart. Had she truly escaped The Ornate Sapphire's grasp, or had they allowed her to leave, knowing she was too broken to ever escape their influence? Were the events—the killings, the experiments, just another layer of manipulation, designed to push her toward this final act? And with that dream, could the life she knew ever be reclaimed? Or was her destiny forever intertwined with these phantoms of violence and guilt?

The whistle of the oncoming train now seemed to echo with the promise of oblivion. Still, a final query gnawed at her: Could someone, somewhere, piece together the truth from the fragments left behind? Might the abandoned notebook on the platform serve as the sole remnant of a secret too monstrous to remain hidden? And if so, would anyone ever make sense of it?

As Lucy stood at the edge of the platform, the train barrelling toward her, Peter's face flashed before her eyes. She saw his vulnerability, his kindness, his desperate need for connection. And she knew, with absolute certainty, that he had never lied to her, that he had truly cared for her, despite everything. A wave of regret washed over her, so intense it nearly knocked her off her feet. 'I was wrong,' she thought. 'He wasn't part of it. He was just trying to help me. And I destroyed him.' The train was almost upon her now, the wind whipping through her hair, the ground trembling beneath her feet. "I'm sorry, Peter," she whispered. "I'm so sorry." And then, in a final act of selflessness, she thought not of escaping her pain, but of freeing Peter from the burden of her memory. She pictured him moving on, finding happiness with someone else, forgetting all about the crazy girl he had met in London. "He deserves that," she thought. "He deserves to be free." And with that thought, she closed her eyes and stepped forward, surrendering to the darkness, hoping that her sacrifice would somehow bring him peace.

Without a backward glance, Lucy stepped to the platform's edge. The ground beneath her was cold and irrevocable.

With a shuddering breath, she closed her eyes, surrendering to the chaos, the voices, the uncertainty. Was this a final rebellion, a desperate attempt to reclaim control? Or was it the ultimate capitulation, the inevitable end point of their twisted game? She didn't know, and perhaps, in the end, it didn't matter. She stepped off into the whirl of uncertainty and steel. The train, a dark silhouette against the pale morning, roared past, consuming her in its relentless momentum.

As onlookers gasped in stunned silence, questions hung in the air like an unfinished refrain: Was this the end of her tragedy or merely another beginning? Could anyone ever tell where reality ended, and delusion began? Had the secrets of The Ornate Sapphire, of London's dark underbelly, just been dispatched along with her, or were they waiting to be discovered in a note carelessly left on the platform?

The platform remained quiet in the aftermath—a stage left behind by a final, enigmatic act that refused to offer answers.

EPILOGUE

The Ornate Sapphire Hotel stood silent against the moor, its secrets buried deep within its walls. The local authorities investigated Lucy's death, deeming it a suicide brought on by a history of mental illness and a recent traumatic experience. Peter's body was never recovered, and his whereabouts remain unknown, leaving a lingering question mark over his involvement in the events at The Ornate Sapphire. The Ornate Sapphire was briefly under investigation, but with no hard evidence of foul play and the residents all offering similar accounts of Lucy and Peter's stay, the case was closed.

The investigation into the death of the homeless man in London was hampered by a lack of evidence and conflicting accounts. While Lucy was initially considered a suspect, the case eventually went cold, leaving unanswered questions about why the couple had been allowed to leave the city without further scrutiny.

The hotel continued to operate, though whispers of strange happenings and unexplained disappearances persisted in area gossip. Over time, these tales became local legend, drawing thrill-seekers and paranormal enthusiasts, unknowingly drawn to the site of unspeakable experiments.

The leather-bound notebook, left on the train platform, was found and filed away as lost property, its contents deemed the ramblings of a disturbed mind. It sat in a dusty storage room for years, until one day, a young journalist stumbled upon it while researching local mysteries. Intrigued by the cryptic entries and unsettling details, she began to investigate. What she found was a rabbit hole of manipulated memories, suppressed truths, and a disturbing legacy that threatened to resurface and consume her as well. A voice of scepticism echoed in her mind.

'What does it mean to be sane, hm? Is it just being someone who agrees with the majority? Or is it something deeper? What if the whole world is a lie?'

In a moment, she paused, deciding whether to continue.

Despite years of rumours and suspicious activity, local authorities never thoroughly investigated The Ornate Sapphire, primarily due to a combination of underfunding, lack of resources, and quiet directives from above ensuring its continued operation. The Ornate Sapphire remained, a silent sentinel guarding its secrets, waiting for the next unsuspecting soul to cross its threshold. Whispers persisted, however, that Project Threshold was protected by figures in high places, their silence bought with promises of influence and access to its dark innovations.

EPILOGUE 2:

Oversights

Maria's story

A strained and somewhat verbally and emotionally abusive relationship with her father (possibly due to alcoholism on the father's part), led to an often withdrawn child going through the motions into adolescence.

She gained a friendship with Lucy in secondary school, and they connected through shared pain in their unhealthy relationship with their fathers'.

At the aftermath of the incidents in London, Maria withdrew more into her shell, deciding to move north of London, eventually settling on Luton due to the cheaper rent. The incident with Lucy triggered depression for Maria, she was confused by Lucy's unexplained sexual confusion at the time, she felt a degree of sexual confusion and felt violated by the incident. But she deeply regretted how she reacted, and didn't know she had that anger inside of her. Maria started to drink heavily because of this. Conflicting thoughts on losing a close friend.

Eventually Maria decided to reach out to Lucy, before discovering what happened to her and the suicide up north. Maria's drinking then got out of control and she became quite promiscuous. She had 3 children with 3 different fathers over a 6 year spell, feeling a detachment from her offspring which mirrors the relationship she had with her parents.

Because of her heavy drinking, Maria would black out for hours at a time, eventually this would result in Maria losing custody of all 3 children. Or did it, was Maria just another manifestation?

Landlord

The manager of the Trout Inn is named Derick Barry. Derick is a 52 year old landlord of the Trout Inn. His backstory, a self-employed Heating Engineer from Carlisle, Derick once owned a thriving plumbing business. His home life was somewhat turbulent due to excessive gambling, which meant his family seldom reaped the rewards from his business.

In a high-stakes poker game, he inadvertently put his business up as a stake. This massively backfired, and he lost control of his company to an unknown associate of David Mercer.

In the following years, he was employed by a local plumbing company. the first couple of months went well, with the employers impressed by the quality of his work. He was well liked by his colleagues, and most of them were unaware of any issues he may have. Soon enough though, Derick would start using cash given to him by customers for the jobs down the bookies after work on horse and dog racing.

The first couple resulted in slight wins, so the company was none the wiser. But within time his addiction would spiral out of control, and he would often stay until the bookies shut or he lost everything.

Slowly his personality changed to an aggressive, bitter, resentful person who only felt alive when he was gambling.

The late nights gambling, and destitute situation with money at home left the family on the brink. After a couple of sympathetic (with his affliction) warnings from his boss, he was fired for stealing from the company. His wife and kids left him, his house was about to be repossessed.

He downloaded a new app on his phone, Sapphire Casinos, and won the deed to a pub (The Trout Inn) in a blackjack game. But despite the name on the deed, the Ornate Sapphire was aware of everything that transpired there and this transaction may have been part of David Mercer's plan regarding the eventual fate of Lucy and Peter.

ACKNOWLEDGEMENTS

Firstly, I'd like to thank my girlfriend Emma for her patience and support in the process of writing this. Without that, I'm not sure Distortion from the truth would have seen a release date.

I'd like to thank all my friends and family who have supported me with the release of this book, this support has included showing genuine interest in the book and helping out with advertising. This help has not gone unnoticed.

Lastly, Joseph Gibbon BA has been instrumental in helping with the polished version you see today. Joe proofread my novel and used his degree in English Literature, to review my novel, identifying sections that needed tightening before release and any plot falls. Whilst he hasn't directly edited the novel, his contribution has helped produce the work you see today.

REFERENCES

Milgram, S. (1963). Behavioral Study of obedience. *The Journal of Abnormal and Social Psychology, 67*(4), 371–378.

Zimbardo, P., Haney, C., Banks, C.W., & Jaffe, D. (1971). Stanford Prison Experiment. https://web.stanford.edu/dept/spec_coll/uarch/exhibits/Narration.pdf

Printed in Dunstable, United Kingdom